FORT SUICIDE

Gordon D. Shirreffs

Inside Fort Joslyn were sixty-seven officers and men, fifty mutinous outcasts and twenty-five helpless women. Outside the fort was a swarm of blood-crazed Apaches. Captain Travis Walker had ridden long and hard to reach the outpost and came face to face with the infamous "Red Knife", the most feared Apache chieftain in the country. The captain was given till sundown to bring out from the fort the supplies that Red Knife said were his, and one woman . . . but that woman belonged to Travis Walker.

Other Large Print Books
by Gordon D. Shirreffs

THE LAST MAN ALIVE
NEVADA GUN

FORT SUICIDE

Gordon D. Shirreffs

Curley Publishing, Inc.
South Yarmouth, Ma.

Library of Congress Cataloging-in-Publication Data

Shirreffs, Gordon D.
    Fort suicide / Gordon D. Shirreffs.
        p.   cm.
    1. Large type books.   I. Title.
    [PS3569.H562F6 1989]
    813'.54—dc20
    ISBN 0–7927–0076–7 (lg. print)   89–35610
    ISBN 0–7927–0077–5 (pbk. : lg. print)   CIP

Published in Large Print by arrangement with Donald MacCampbell, Inc. in the United States, Canada, the U.K. and British Commonwealth.

Distributed in Great Britain, Ireland and the Commonwealth by CHIVERS LIBRARY SERVICES LIMITED, Bath BA1 3HB, England.

Printed in Great Britain

FORT SUICIDE

CHAPTER ONE

Travis Walker squatted in the hot shade of a rock outcropping high in the side of a mesa that thrust itself up from the flat floor of the New Mexican desert. Far below him he could see the winding ruts of the old military road which led to Fort Joslyn. The desert and mesa seemed empty of human life, but instinct and long experience in the Southwest warned him that this was the very time to look for Apaches. They would watch and wait until the right time for an ambush occurred; then and then only, would they be seen by their intended victims.

The metal of his Sharps carbine was almost too hot for his hands, so he set it aside after checking the cap on the nipple. The rock at his feet burned through the thin soles of his worn boots. The long miles from the valley of the San Pedro down across the border into Sonora, then across the Continental Divide which separated Sonora from Chihuahua, had played hell with his horse and with him.

He had crossed over from Chihuahua into New Mexico Territory before dawn that morning, knowing he would strike the Fort

Joslyn road north of Big Hatchet Peak. It would have been easier for him to strike north up the valley of the San Pedro and reach the old Butterfield Trail, but in the early summer of 1861 all Federal troops had abandoned their posts and stations in Arizona to retreat to the Rio Grande, leaving eastern Arizona and western New Mexico open to the ravages of Cochise and his Chiricahuas and Mangus Colorado and his Mimbrenos. So Travis Walker, captain of United States Cavalry, had taken the longest but safest way around to report for duty at Fort Craig on the Rio Grande.

Travis eyed the flapping toe of his left boot. He pulled his dirty bandanna from about his throat and bound it about the boot toe. He had done more walking over rough country in the past week than he had done in the eight years of his service in the Southwest.

He waited with the patience of an Apache until the long shadows fell across the slopes of the mesa. Travis shook his canteen, and was about to swill his remaining water when he thought of his horse. It took all the will he had to carry the canteen to where he had picketed his rangy bay. Boots whinnied softly when he saw Travis. He shoved his nose against Travis' dusty shirt and rubbed at it.

Travis grinned. "Look, hardhead," he said,

"I'll be wearing a uniform again in a few days."

Travis took off his hat and poured the remaining water into it. He held the hat toward the horse, and Boots drank. Travis put on his hat, grateful for the temporary coolness of the wet fabric. He led his bay to the rock outcropping, then attached his carbine to the snap ring on the saddle.

The darkening desert was still deserted. He led the horse down the long slope, taking advantage of every scrap of cover. A velvety darkness had fallen when he reached the desert floor. A cool wind fingered about him as he struck off for the dim bulk of Big Hatchet Peak.

There was one thought in Travis Walker's mind as he plodded toward the peak – to get back to the Army and fight against the Confederacy. He had entered West Point at the age of eighteen and had graduated nineteenth in the Class of 1849. Since then, *U.S.* had been branded on his lean flank just as it had been on the flanks of the cavalry company he had commanded at Fort Yuma until April of '61. He had missed the Mexican War, but from all reports this new war promised to outdo that recent affair by far, and Travis Walker meant to get into it.

There would be no moon this night, but Big

Hatchet Peak would be his beacon. He crossed the Fort Joslyn road, and as his boots sank into the deep ruts he thought again that perhaps Fort Joslyn had been abandoned as so many other Southwestern posts had been. Perhaps the Confederates had come up from Texas and had occupied it.

Travis led the bay half a mile beyond the road, then mounted him. He placed his carbine across his thighs and loosened his Navy Colt in its holster. He rode steadily, with his gray eyes sweeping the terrain all about him. Apaches didn't like night fighting, for a warrior killed at night might wander forever trying to find The House of Spirits, speaking through the melancholy voice of Bu, the owl. Still, if he blundered into some of them they'd fight like the skilled warriors they were.

It was midnight by his watch when he called a halt high on the slopes of the Hatchet Mountains. The big bay was tired. He picketed Boots in a draw which afforded the horse some sparse grazing. He himself gnawed at some dried venison he had purchased from a Mexican ranchero. The man had thrown in a bottle of Baconora mezcal for good measure. Travis finished his frugal meal and allowed himself two dollops of mezcal. The potent liquor seemed to put new life into him.

He looked to the north, up the valley

4

between the Hatchets and the dim Cedar Mountains. Suddenly he saw a spurt of yellow light on the valley floor, then it was gone as quickly as it had come. There was life down there.

"What kind of life?" he asked himself aloud.

Fort Joslyn was down there somewhere. Maybe a sentry had risked taking a smoke on duty. If it wasn't a member of the garrison who had struck that light then it could only be an Apache.

He looked to the east. He was at least a hundred miles from the Rio Grande. There was plenty of water between him and the river. The only trouble was that the water was contained in waterholes, many miles apart, and every one of those waterholes were known to the Apaches like the palms of their greasy hands. There was good water at Fort Joslyn and at the little *placita* of Santa Theresa some miles north of the outpost. But, if Fort Joslyn had been abandoned, that would also mean that Santa Theresa would be a ghost town, haunted by the predatory Mimbrenos.

Travis unbuckled his cantle pack and removed his uniform from it. He shook his head as he eyed the wrinkles in the good material. He'd be a helluva-looking yellowleg when he rode onto the first occupied post he could find. Travis spread the blanket on the ground and lay flat on it, with his Sharps between his right arm and his body. He looked down into the dark valley as though he could penetrate the darkness with his eyes. Travis fell asleep with an uneasiness which refused to leave him.

The bay whinnied softly, and Travis was awake in an instant. He got to his feet and snatched up his carbine. He padded down the slope to the bay and spoke softly to it. He was ready to cut off its wind instantly if the bay tried to whinny again.

There was a faint trace of light in the eastern sky, but he wasn't sure if it was the new moon or the coming of the false dawn. He waited there with a trickle of cold sweat working its way down from each armpit.

The bay raised its head, and Travis clamped a big hand on its windpipe. The bay shied a little. Travis looked down the slope. There was a movement in the darkness. Dim mounted figures materialized from amongst the brush. There were six of them looking up the slope toward Travis. Then suddenly they were gone as quickly as they had come. No troopers nor Mexican travelers could move as silently as those mysterious horsemen had done.

6

Travis backed away from the bay and went to his camp. Swiftly he rolled his cantle pack and took it back to the bay. He buckled it in place and then walked away from the horse to listen. The wind moaned softly through the brush. The thudding of his heart interfered with his listening. Mentally he calculated the risk. If there were only six of them he had a chance of holding off a rush. But there were some alternatives. They could wait until he went down into the valley and then ambush him or close in on him. They could surround his camp and hold him there until thirst and heat softened him for the kill.

The night had been quiet before, but now it seemed alive with a myriad of soft and indistinguishable sounds. The wind sighed, and the brush rubbed against rocks. Something scuttled for cover down the western slope. Travis wet his cracked lips. They could move as noiselessly as cats. He had once been on patrol from Fort Yuma into the brooding Kofas. They had found three prospectors dead in their bloodstained blankets, with sightless eyes staring at the dawn sky. Their throats had been slashed from ear to ear. Their horses, mules and equipment had been taken, and all the Cocopah scouts had found were the tracks of only one warrior about the camp. Probably none of the three murdered men had had a chance to awaken for their last living breath.

Now the brush seemed alive with prowling figures, razor-edged *besh* in their strong hands, closing in on Travis Walker. He fought down the slimy green panic which tried to flow over his mind. His bowels seemed to churn within him.

The eastern sky was lighter now, and he could distinguish the distant peaks. In a short time he would be exposed to a carefully aimed rifle shot – a crippling shot that would leave him helpless in the hands of the Apaches. They would have their sport before they finished him off.

Boots moved restlessly. His hoofs clashed on the rock, causing a cold sweat to break out on Travis' forehead. A white man could have heard the din half a mile off. Boots raised his head, then shied and blew. There was a devil's ring closing in on the hilltop. Dawn was the time for killing.

Travis swung upon the bay and laid the steel into his flanks. The bay reared and plunged, then shot down the dim slope. A rifle shot shattered the quietness not fifty feet behind Travis. He bent low in the saddle and spurred for his life. He saw the ledge just in time to lift the bay over it. Boots came down hard, lost his stride, then crashed pell-mell through

8

a clinging thicket of catclaw which raked through Travis' trousers like red-hot needles.

A ululating cry broke out behind Travis, driven up from the Apache's diaphragm and pistoned out of his square mouth. Travis did not dare look back as he made his breakneck descent of the treacherous slope, gripping the reins with his left and his Sharps with his right hand. Rifles popped behind him and he felt something pluck at his hat.

Boots hit the level ground and broke into his long swinging stride. There were great coils of power in the haunches of the big cavalry gelding, coupled with a sure eye for holes and loose stones, and Travis knew the bay could outrun most Apache mounts for a time. But they would try to wear down the bay. Travis dared to look back. The bucks had broken into the clear too. Half a dozen of them, driving their wiry mounts as though they had been born part of them. The pursuers separated. Four of them stayed behind Travis while the other two began to forge ahead at top speed, one on each flank, forming the dread pursuit crescent.

The strategy was old. Travis had seen Cocopahs and Yumas run down rabbits the same way by keeping some of the runners behind the quarry while others came up alongside it, driving it to its utmost frantic speed, forcing it from one side to the other so that it covered more ground than its pursuers, while the rear party kept up the steady pressure behind it.

Travis cocked his Sharps. He dropped the reins on Boots' neck and swung in his saddle. He raised his carbine and led the left hand buck a little, then lowered the muzzle to get a bead on the buck's wiry claybank. He squeezed off. The Sharps jerked back against his shoulder, and he saw the claybank go down, pitching his rider far in front of him. The Apache hit the ground running.

There was no time to reload the Sharps. Travis snapped it to its sling and then freed his Navy Colt. The Fort Joslyn road trended from the west. He spurred the bay until he was racing down the high center of the road. Boots kept up his steady pace, but he was tossing at the bit. The rear party was gaining steadily. The right flank warrior closed in. He leveled rifle and fired, but missed. Travis looked for the warrior to draw a hand gun, but instead he whipped a war club up from where it hung at his waist. The rear warriors began to fire to rattle Travis.

The hard-riding warrior was twenty feet from Travis now. "Trying to make a blasted hero of himself," said Travis aloud. Travis fired, but the warrior threw himself on the far side of his run, leaving exposed only a moccasined foot hooked on the near side of the dun and a hand gripping the shaggy mane. Still he gained on Travis.

Travis looked ahead. There was something on the valley floor. It looked like a handful of children's blocks. He knew it for Fort Joslyn, but there was no sign of life there. He passed the burned remains of three wagons. Three bloated horses lay to one side, with strips of flesh hacked from them. There wasn't much doubt in Travis' mind about it being Apache work, and that done within sight of the fort. It was a sure sign that the fort had been abandoned.

Boots' head was outstretched. His breath was rasping. Foam from the weakening bay's mouth struck Travis' face. The warrior lanced in for the kill, drawing his war club back for a smashing blow at man or horse. Travis switched his Colt to his left hand, dropped the reins and whipped his saber free from its sheath. He caught the surprised warrior with a backhand stroke that sheared through the tough handle of the war club and struck hard against the warrior's head. He went down as though poleaxed.

A rifle cracked from behind. Boots faltered in his stride. He'd never make it to the shelter of the post walls. Travis shot a glance back at his pursuers. They were sixty yards behind him and gaining fast. There was no sign of life at the fort as Travis turned to look at it. There was only one thing to do – his last drawing card in the swift game of death. He freed his left foot from its stirrup, sheathed his saber, and gripped the forward edge of his saddle with his free hand. Then he fired the Navy Colt inches from the rear of Boots' head. As the big bay went down Travis leaped from the saddle to clear the horse. Boots smashed against the ground, jerked a little and then lay still.

Travis dropped behind the dead horse and rested his right hand on the bay to steady his aim. He had four shots left. He gripped his right wrist with his left hand and sighted over the hammer notch. A brown chest swam into view, and he squeezed off. Smoke blew back into his face as he cocked the big hand gun, but through it he saw the Apache fall.

The last three bucks swerved aside, throwing themselves on the far side of their horses. They raced to the west, trailing a cloud of dust behind them.

Travis rested his head on the sweaty body of the bay. The reaction from the fight flooded over him. He forced himself to free his carbine from the bay and load it. The warriors were out of sight in the thick brush, but a scarf of dust revealed their passage. Travis loaded his Colt and then bent to cut his gear loose from the bay. His head jerked back as he heard the familiar notes of a big infantry G bugle break the valley quiet, to be instantly followed by the brazen notes of a cavalry C trumpet.

Travis turned slowly. He was no more than a quarter of a mile from the adobe buildings of Fort Joslyn. The post stood out clearly in the dawn light, and even as he watched he saw lamplight brighten the windows. A shower of sparks shot out of a chimney, followed by a puff of smoke that trailed off in a streamer before the shifting dawn wind. The wind had been blowing directly toward the fort, and surely, if a sleepy sentry hadn't seen the fighting on the road, he would have heard the shooting.

Travis raised his carbine and fired it. The report flatted off. A moment later he saw a man come out from between two buildings and look toward him. He reloaded and fired again. Then he sat down on the dead bay.

It was twenty minutes after Travis had been seen that a squad of horsemen broke from the fort and trotted toward him through the thick brush until they reached the road. An officer led them with a drawn saber in his hand.

Travis stood up as the officer halted his

squad fifty yards away. "Who are you?" called out the officer.

"Captain Travis Walker, United States Army."

"What are you doing out here?"

"Looking at the God-damned scenery!" roared Travis. "Come over here, mister! I'm not in the mood to make conversation across fifty yards of space!"

The officer rode forward, followed by his squad. The bare shoulder straps of a second lieutenant were on his shoulders. He stared at Travis and then at the dead bay. "I'm Second Lieutenant Norval DeSantis," he said. "Second United States Dragoons on detached duty here at Fort Joslyn."

Despite his anger, Travis felt relieved that Fort Joslyn was still occupied by United States troops. "You must be wide awake, Mr. DeSantis," he snapped. "Six Apaches chased me this far from those hills, shooting at me and getting shot at, and not a soul stirred in your precious fort."

DeSantis flushed. He sheathed his fine saber. "I have just your word on that, sir!" he said hotly.

Travis thudded his carbine butt against the ground. "You'll see a downed Apache twenty yards up the road if you'll look," he said.

DeSantis spurred forward, then reined his

14

fine black in sharply as he saw the buck lying in the brush. He swung down quickly and walked toward the warrior. He was five feet from the Apache when the warrior came to swift violent life. A knife flashed upward in his hand. DeSantis jumped back, caught a spur in a root and went down. The Apache jumped up and raised his knife. Travis freed his Colt from its sheath and fired twice. The warrior spun about and went down, clawing at the ground.

Travis hurdled his dead horse and raced toward DeSantis. The warrior was still thrashing on the ground. He turned his head to look at Travis and began to sing his death song in a husky voice. *"O ha le! O ha le . . ."* The crashing report of the Colt cut short his song. The bullet had hit him squarely between the eyes.

Travis blew the smoke from his Colt.

"For God's sake!" husked DeSantis. "You never gave him a chance! We could have taken him prisoner!"

Travis grinned crookedly. "How long have you been out on the frontier, mister?"

"Three months."

Travis holstered his Colt and nodded. "Still wet behind the ears, too. No experienced soldier would have walked up on a buck like that. They're experts at playing possum, and the wounded ones won't surrender. What were

15

you looking for? A brevet for bringing in a live Apache?"

DeSantis flushed as the barbed verbal shaft drove home. An intense hatred of the sunburned, whiskered man before him was conceived at that instant.

A corporal cantered up. He saluted Travis. "We've got your saddle and equipment, sir," he said. He looked down at the dead warrior and then at DeSantis. "The captain sure saved your life, sir. You didn't have a chance."

DeSantis got up and dusted off his fine broadcloth uniform. He waited until a trooper rode up and gave his horse to Travis. Travis mounted and the trooper slogged back through the sand to mount behind one of his mates. Travis and DeSantis rode to the squad. DeSantis took his place at the head of the detail and rode toward the fort. The corporal looked at Travis. "You had a close call, sir," he said.

"Does your commanding officer allow Apaches to raid within half a mile of the post?"

The corporal shrugged. "Major Lester has his problems, sir."

"What about those three wagons back there on the road?"

The corporal shrugged. "Those were Mex wagons being driven to Santa Theresa.

Cuchillo Rojo struck them three days ago while the garrison was standing retreat. We heard the shooting and saw the smoke. We buried five Mex men in the post cemetery. One of them lived long enough to tell us there had been two women and a fifteen-year-old girl with the wagons. The captain knows what probably happened to them."

Travis placed a hand on his cantle and looked back down the road. "How many Apaches did the garrison get?"

The noncom laughed harshly. "We didn't go out until the Apaches were gone. The only trace we found of them was fresh horse manure. Maybe some day we'll run across the bodies of those three Mex women. I hope I *never* see them."

Travis looked ahead as the detail skirted the fort and turned in toward the gate, which was nothing more than a wide space between two buildings. What kind of a commanding officer was Major Lester, to let those three wagons get shot up and burned within eyesight of the post and do nothing about it?

"Cuchillo Rojo?" he said. "Mimbreno?"

The corporal nodded. "One of Mangus Colorado's fighting chiefs. One of the best damned guerrillas and raiders in this God-forsaken part of the Southwest."

Travis looked at the hills, now being lit by

17

the rays of the rising sun. Cuchillo Rojo . . .
Red Knife. There was no need to ask how he
had earned his name.

CHAPTER TWO

Fort Joslyn could hardly be called more than
military camp. The post was formed by a
rectangle of adobe and fieldstone buildings in
poor repair. Troopers and infantrymen looked
curiously at Travis as he swung down from his
horse and slapped the dust from his clothing
with his battered Kossuth hat. The rising sun
shone on the barrel of a stubby brass howitzer
which stood near the warped flagpole.

Norval DeSantis saluted Travis. "The
major is in his quarters," he said.

"I'll wait for him in his office, mister."

DeSantis hesitated. "The major hasn't been
feeling well," he said with a faint tinge of
sarcasm in his voice. "He'll probably want to
see you in his quarters."

Travis nodded. The young lieutenant led
the way to a large adobe structure and opened
the door for Travis. Travis walked into a dim
hallway, and his nose was instantly assailed by
the pungent odor of some kind of medicine

18

or ointment. DeSantis wrinkled his nose as he opened another door and ushered Travis in ahead of him.

The medicinal odor in the big hot room made Travis' eyes water. A pudgy man wearing a thick flannel nightgown sat on a rumpled bed, his feet immersed in a steaming pan of water. A fire blazed in a whitewashed beehive fireplace in one corner of the room. A trooper was busily rubbing the pudgy man's neck and shoulders.

"Well, DeSantis," snapped the pudgy man. "What is it? What is it?"

DeSantis saluted. "One of our sentries heard firing south of the fort. Captain Cass sent me out to investigate. I found this man out there. His horse had been downed, and he had driven off an Apache attack. He says he is Captain Travis Walker of the United States Army."

Travis saluted. "I assume you are Major Lester, sir?"

The man nodded. "Major Enos Lester, Corps of Quartermasters, officer commanding Fort Joslyn, Department of New Mexico."

Travis eyed the man. Even in a uniform Major Enos Lester would not be imposing. His skull was bald and pink, with a ruff of grayish white hair standing up about it. His pale blue eyes were weak and watery.

"You have proof that you are an army officer?" demanded Lester. "Shut that damned door, DeSantis! Do you want me to catch my death of cold?" He looked back over his shoulder. "Rub harder, Kelligan!"

"Yes, sir!"

Travis took out his orders and silently passed them to Enos Lester. The major took a pair of brass-bound spectacles from a table and adjusted them on his pulpy nose. He peered at the orders. "On special detached duty in Arizona, eh? Well then, sir! What are you doing here?"

Travis raised his head. The man sounded like a pettish old woman who had been disturbed while feeding her cat. "If the major will read the attached sheet he will see that my orders, at the completion of my mission, are to report to the commanding officer of the Department of New Mexico. I did not care to risk traveling to New Mexico via the Butterfield Trail, so I passed into Sonora, then east to Chihuahua, thence north here to Fort Joslyn. I traveled in civilian clothing to avoid suspicion. However I brought my uniform with me."

Lester folded the orders and tapped on them with a blunt forefinger. "What was the nature of your special detached duty?"

Travis looked at the orderly and then at

DeSantis. "It is of a confidential nature, sir."

Lester waved a hand. "Out with the both of you!" he snapped. He waited until the door closed behind DeSantis and Kelligan. "Well, Walker?"

Travis loosened his collar a little. Sweat was pouring from his body. The temperature in the room was at least ninety degrees. "We received information at Fort Yuma that certain Regular Army officers, still in our uniform, were traveling through Arizona, inciting enlisted men to desert and join the Confederacy. We also heard that there were certain citizens of some prominence in Arizona who were planning to give aid and comfort to the enemy should they invade that territory. My orders were to track some of them down and gather the necessary information on them to have them brought to trial for treason."

"And you succeeded?"

"To some extent."

"Show me your information."

"It is memorized, sir. Certain incriminating papers have been cached near Tucson to be repossessed when Federal troops return there to take control of the territory again."

Lester snorted. "That will take some time. We have heard that Confederate troops are forming in Texas to invade New Mexico. At

21

the present time the department commander is strengthening Fort Craig on the Rio Grande for the purpose of stopping a Texas invasion of the Rio Grande Valley. My post, sir, is the only post still under the United States flag between the Rio Grande and the Colorado."

"A tough assignment," said Travis.

"It is indeed, sir." Lester shrugged his damp nightgown up about his shoulders and swilled medicine from a square black bottle. "I am a sick man, Captain Walker, with almost forty years of service behind me. I have been more or less abandoned here in the Apache country with inadequate supplies, outmoded weapons, a ragtag and bobtail set of officers and enlisted men, and with no one to give me advice but God himself. And I may add, sir, my prayers have not been too successful!"

"I hope they will be, sir. Now, with your permission, I'll draw a horse from your quartermaster officer and continue on to the Rio Grande."

Lester stood up. "Put some more wood on that damned fire so that I can dress in comfort."

Travis did as he was bid. Lester peeled off his gown, revealing a potbelly and bandy legs. He pulled on long underwear and then dressed himself in full uniform, buckling on his sword belt. He hastily brushed back his muff of hair and placed a velvet-trimmed Kossuth hat on his head. He pulled the brim down over his eyes. "An officer on frontier duty must always look smart in front of his men," he said.

My God, thought Travis, the look of an eagle. The heat of a summer day in that country was enough to fell a man wearing a flannel shirt.

"You have had much frontier service?" asked Lester.

"Eight years, sir. Class of '49, then duty in New Mexico, Texas and Arizona ever since."

"In eight years you've made a captaincy? Surely it is a brevet rank?"

"No, sir."

Enos Lester shook his head. "And me with forty years of service behind me and still a major. Discrimination, sir. Politicking by desk officers in Washington. I had hoped to get my brigade if my health improved. The drums of war are fine music to my ears, Captain."

"I have no doubt about that, Major," said Travis politely.

"Eight years' frontier service and a captain at your age. I could use you here, sir."

"I have my orders, Major Lester."

"So you do, and I have *mine*. Suppose we go to my office and talk things over?"

Travis looked suspiciously at the bumbling little man as he opened the door and waited until Lester passed into the hallway. There was something in Lester's tone that Travis didn't like.

The outer air, warm though it was, struck Travis like a cool draft after leaving Lester's room. Half a dozen ramshackle wagons were grouped at one end of the post quadrangle. As Travis eyed them he saw a buxom woman step over the tailgate of one of them, revealing a long expanse of shapely legs clad in red-and-white striped stockings. A passing trooper whistled. The woman turned and giggled. Another woman eyed the trooper and flirted her hips at him. Some civilian men squatted beside a building, drinking from tin mugs. A line of wash was strung from one wagon to another, and women's underwear waved in the warm breeze.

Major Lester pointed at the wagons. "Refugees," he said offhand. "I have given them protection here. They are awaiting a chance to make the Rio Grande."

"A rough-looking lot," observed Travis.

"Perhaps. But they *are* United States citizens. It is my duty to protect them."

Travis nodded. With women like that, on a crowded post surrounded by women-starved troopers, the post took on an air of a powder keg with someone waving a lighted cigar over it. He had experienced situations like this before during Indian scares.

Some of the troopers saluted Lester as he passed, and Travis was sure he caught a glint of amusement in their eyes. The more he saw of Fort Joslyn the more he wished he was watering his horse in the Rio Grande.

Lester paraded pompously into his office and hung his Kossuth hat on a hood. "Sit down, Walker," he invited.

Travis sat down. Lester shoved a box of cigars toward him. "Help yourself. They do my sinuses no good."

Travis lit up one of the dry cigars. He eyed a picture of General Winfield Scott which hung on the wall behind Lester's desk. Lester glanced up at it. Thinking he had resembled Old Fuss and Feathers in his younger days filled him with pride.

"Now about *your* orders," said Lester. "I'm afraid they have been superseded, shall we say?"

Travis shot a look at the major. "Superseded? By whom? They came directly from Santa Fe last June."

Lester waved a pudgy hand. "I know that, Walker. I saw the signature and date at the bottom. But times have changed in the department. Not a month ago I received an

25

order – a blanket order, shall we say, which certainly supersedes those you have."

There was a cold feeling in Travis' gut. The pompous little rooster wasn't joking. Joking was probably something Enos Lester never did. It might deflate the dignity of forty years' service and the gold oak leaf on his shoulder strap.

Drill Call sounded out on the parade ground as Lester fumbled through a stack of papers in a basket on his desk. Then, with a triumphant air, he withdrew a sheet. "Read this," he said with a tight little smile.

Travis scanned through it. It was an order to the effect that all officers and enlisted men, who had no definite assignment and were separated from other commands, would report to the nearest camp, post or station of the United States Army for such duty as would be prescribed by the commanding officer of any such camp, post or station, until orders were received from the department commander ordering them elsewhere.

Travis looked up at Enos Lester. "This can't apply to me," he said quietly.

"No? Are you a guardhouse lawyer, sir?"

Travis bit his lip, holding back a retort that would sting the pudgy little man like a giant Sonoran ant. "My orders were to report to the department commander at Santa Fe when

26

I had completed my mission. My mission has been completed, and I am on my way to the Rio Grande."

"So?" Lester steepled his fingers and rested his wrists on his chest. He leaned back in his chair and idly swung it back and forth. He seemed perfectly at home in his swivel chair. Travis wondered whether he'd be as much at home in a McClellan saddle, leading his hoped-for brigade. "You were driven here by Apaches. The country between here and the Rio Grande is probably swarming with more of them."

"I can get through by traveling at night."

"Alone? I can't spare you a squad, sir!"

Travis waved a big hand. "A company couldn't get through perhaps, but one man, traveling as I do, has a good chance of doing so."

"What makes you think so?"

Travis smiled faintly. "I rode alone from Fort Yuma to Tucson, from there to the Sonoran border, then to Fort Joslyn."

Lester dropped his hands to his sides and let his chair swing him upward. He smashed a hand down on the desk with the obvious intention of startling Travis, but he had mistaken his man. Travis relit his cigar and eyed Lester through the bluish smoke. "You will remain here under my orders, sir!"

snapped the major. His voice broke a little.

"And if I don't, sir?"

Lester extended a forefinger. "I will *prevent* you from leaving."

The little puffed-up toad had Travis by the short hairs, and he knew it.

Travis leaned back in his chair. There would come a day when Major Enos Lester, Quartermaster Corps, commanding Fort Joslyn, Department of New Mexico would have to face his commanding officer and explain how he had countermanded his superior officer's orders. Until that time, Travis Walker would sweat out the days, weeks and perhaps months under Enos Lester's command. It wasn't a pleasant prospect to look forward to, for Travis had learned plenty about Fort Joslyn and Enos Lester in the short experience he had had with both of them.

Lester smiled. "I'm sorry I have to be so abrupt," he said, "but I am in dire straits here, and I could use a man of your experience."

Travis nodded.

"I have sixty men and five officers here. The men are a mixture of infantry, quartermaster, dragoons and cavalry. I have one gun section composed of dragoons to man my one mountain howitzer. Captain Charles Cass commands the infantry; First Lieutenant

Clinton Vaughn is post quartermaster; First Lieutenant Kenneth Carlie commands the mounted men with Second Lieutenant Norval DeSantis as his second in command, also in charge of the howitzer section; Second Lieutenant Martin Newkirk is my adjutant."

"That makes seven officers for sixty men. Quite a large percentage, isn't it, sir, for a one-company post, while officers are needed to command units which may have to fight battles against the Confederate States Army?"

Lester flushed. "By Heaven, sir, you try me! I have this post to defend as well as protecting the people of Santa Theresa. My post of command is vital to the peace of New Mexico Territory, and don't you ever forget it, sir!"

Travis bowed his head. "I apologize Major."

"Apology accepted!" snapped Lester. "You will act as my executive officer. The sergeant-major will make out the order. You will see Mr. Vaughn in regards to quarters and equipment. You will present yourself in uniform at the officers' mess for the midday meal, to meet your fellow officers."

Travis stood up. "Yes, sir."

Then the little man went through one of his surprising changes. He stood up and extended his hand. "Glad to have you with us, Walker."

29

Travis gripped the soft damp hand. "Glad to be with you, sir."

Travis walked outside and looked at the cigar in his hand. He threw it on the ground and stamped on it, then walked toward the quartermaster warehouse to find Lieutenant Vaughn. The post looked sloppy and the men down-at-the-heels. There was a general air of decay and low morale about Fort Joslyn. It was nothing specific, but Travis had learned in eight years to sense the inner feelings of men and frontier posts; and this God-forsaken collection of sagging adobes and cracking fieldstone buildings was the worst – by far – he had ever experienced. God help the United States Army in New Mexico if this was representative of their strength.

CHAPTER THREE

The quartermaster warehouse of Fort Joslyn was a long, sagging adobe. Seeds had caught root on the thick roof, and the building had a curiously shaggy effect from the wild growth there. Travis shook his head. A detail should have cleaned off that mess of a roof long ago, but the appearance of the warehouse was in keeping with the rest of the post.

"Looking for someone, Captain?" a low-throated feminine voice asked from behind Travis.

Travis turned. The woman was so close behind him he almost bumped into her. He stepped back. She was in her early twenties, and well-formed – almost too well-formed. Her bold green eyes studied Travis from head to foot.

"I was just about to enter the warehouse," said Travis.

She smiled. "I thought I could help you."

Travis looked past the woman. Two troopers were polishing the little brass mountain howitzer and eying Travis and the woman with obvious delight.

"I'm Maggie Gillis," she said. "You're new here, ain't you?"

Travis nodded.

"You staying here awhile?"

"Until I can leave for the Rio Grande."

She tucked away a strand of her reddish blonde hair. "You going alone to the Rio Grande?"

"I hope to."

"It's a lonely trip for a man."

"I prefer it that way, ma'am."

"*Ma'am?*" She raised her eyebrows in

31

surprise, then laughed. "Thanks, soldier!"

"You're from the post?"

"God forbid! I came in with a wagon train from the west and been stuck here ever since. What a hole!"

"I'll agree to that."

Travis felt a little uncomfortable. She was as bold as a jay, and quite unconcerned about anyone watching her. "Sure is dead around here. Old Enos Lester tries to keep us civilians around our own camp, but it ain't easy with handsome officers walking about. A girl has to have *some* social life."

I'll bet you do, thought Travis. There was a strong aura of sweat and cheap perfume clinging about the young woman. He looked past her to a tall, lean civilian watching them from the shade of a wagon. The man was paring his nails with a thin-bladed knife, but his eyes were more on Travis than they were on his fingernails.

Travis touched the brim of his hat. "Good morning to you, ma'am," he said.

She pouted. "Ain't I good enough for you to talk to?"

"If that's your husband watching us from over there, you'd better get about your business."

She glanced at the lean civilian. "Him? That's Ben Joad, and he *ain't* my husband."

Travis turned on a heel. "You'd better stay out of the sun," he said over his shoulder. "It does strange things to the mind."

She planted her hands on her full hips. "Damn you!" she said.

Travis grinned as he walked into the warehouse. His grin faded as he heard the two troopers guffaw.

An officer looked up from a littered desk. "Morning, sir," he said.

"You're Clinton Vaughn?"

"Yes." Vaughn stood up.

"Captain Travis Walker. Major Lester has ordered me to stay here on temporary duty. You are to issue me quarters and any equipment I may need." Travis gripped Vaughn's hand.

Vaughn's gray eyes studied Travis. "I have a feeling you won't like it here, Captain."

"That's neither here nor there, mister."

The quartermaster smiled. "No. What will you need in the way of equipment?"

"Nothing much. My horse was killed in my attempt to get to the post. I have my uniform. It needs mending and pressing, but it will do.

"One of the women will attend to that. Maggie Gillis is a good seamstress when she wants to be."

Travis shot a hard look at Vaughn. He had a feeling the man was laughing at him.

Vaughn filled his pipe. "I saw her talking to you outside, sir."

"So?"

"She's a bold one. She seems to take a perverse delight in badgering officers, particularly those she thinks are real men."

Vaughn lit his pipe. He eyed Travis through the smoke. "That was a helluva fight you put up getting here, sir. Corporal Cole told me about it. Major Lester doesn't think much of having patrols out – as a result the Mimbrenos raid right up to within gunshot of the post. We're practically in a state of siege here. In a way it can't be helped. We're the only garrison between here and the Colorado, from what I've heard."

"You're right."

"You probably want to clean up. About quarters ... Captain Cass is married and has his wife here; Ken Carlie has a small room in the officer's barracks, while DeSantis and Newkirk bunk together. I have a large double room with an extra cot in it. If it's all right with you, you can bunk with me. If not, I'll move in with Carlie and let you have the room by yourself."

Travis waved a hand. "I don't want to put you out, Vaughn."

Vaughn put on his forage cap and slanted it to one side. "There's one other alternative

34

– Major Lester occupies one part of a double set of quarters. The quarters across the hall are not used." The gray eyes studied Travis.

Travis shook his head. "I'm used to bunking with someone else. I'd rather have it that way."

Vaughn nodded. "It's just as well. Major Lester has his furniture, spare clothing, books and other gear in the quarters across from him. It's quite full, I assure you."

"I can imagine."

Vaughn looked about his crowded warehouse. Dust motes danced in the rays of sunlight that came through the little high windows. "Quite a store," he said.

"You seem well supplied."

Vaughn grinned. "Weevily hardtack, wormy embalmed beef, bacon as hard as lignum vitae, ammunition issued right after the Mexican War. Jennifer and Grimsley saddles with cracked forks and rotting leather. Chicopee sabers pitted with rust. As far as I know, we're the only troops in the department still carrying muzzleloading Enfield carbines."

Travis raised his head. "You have no breechloaders?"

"A few. In fact, the Mimbrenos are armed mostly with good Sharps carbines, better equipment than we have."

"A nice situation."

Vaughn nodded. "Let's go to my quarters. Get cleaned up and tell me what equipment you need, and I'll have it brought over later."

They left the warehouse. A buxom woman planted herself in front of Vaughn. "You did not send over a carpenter, Mr. Vaughn! My front door is sagging on its hinges, and my back door won't open."

Vaughn held up a hand. "Now, Mrs. Reilly! I told your husband he could have the use of all the tools he needed to do the job."

Mrs. Reilly thrust out her chin. "And poor Pat down with a misery in his back? Are we not as good people as the Army people?"

"I'm sure you are, Mrs. Reilly."

"Then you'll see to it a man comes at once?"

Vaughn shrugged. "All right."

Mrs. Reilly stamped off. Vaughn shook his head. *"Poor* Pat is as healthy as a hog. These civilians have been nothing but trouble since they been staying here."

"Quartermasters are a sorry lot, Clint."

Vaughn nodded. "Sore-tailed from sitting on a hard seat in a dusty warehouse, listening to the drilling of the weevils in the hardtack. Storekeeper, plumber, architect, clerk, wagon master, chaplain and target for every inspecting officer. I wish I was a private in the rear rank of a fighting infantry company."

Ben Joad was leaning against a wagon watching them. Maggie Gillis sat on a keg beside the man, her bedraggled dress open as far down as frontier modesty would permit.

"Who is Ben Joad?" asked Travis.

"Border scum. He claims he's a trapper and scout. Personally, I believe what I've heard about him. They say he was a scalp hunter and raider with Mexican bandits. Men walk quietly around Ben Joad. I never could stand a man who fought with a knife instead of a pistol. I suppose it doesn't really make any difference. After all, it's a means to an end."

"True enough," said Travis dryly.

Vaughn opened the door to his quarters and ushered Travis in ahead of him. The quarters were spacious, with a large beehive fireplace in one corner. Two bunks were neatly made up. Gear hung from pegs driven into the walls, and a shelf of books hung over a desk. An Apache lance hung over the fireplace. Travis touched it. "You've done much Indian fighting?" he asked.

"Enough to dislike it. I got that fighting near Cook's Peak. Rather curious thing. The blade is made from an old French saber. I often wondered where the buck got it from."

"How many of the other officers have had experience in fighting Indians?"

"Captain Cass has had some. Ken Carlie did

some fighting against Lipans and Comanches in Texas. DeSantis is as green as grass. Marty Newkirk just came out from the East before the war started."

"And the major?"

Vaughn knocked out his pipe and felt for his tobacco pouch.

"Well?"

"The major talks a lot about his forty years' service. He knows his regulations."

"You didn't answer my question."

Vaughn turned and looked Travis full in the face. "He claims he has fought Seminoles."

"But that was twenty-five years ago!"

"The captain is getting the idea."

"But he has seen quite a bit of frontier service, hasn't he?"

Vaughn lit his pipe. "As I said, Major Lester knows his regulations. His health hasn't been too good for some years. He was originally an infantryman, but most of his service has been in the Quartermaster Corps and in various staff and paper-work assignments. He was allowed to accompany his regiment to Mexico with Scott's command. Ill health was given as the reason. Captain Cass thinks differently. Cass says every time pressure is put on Lester he becomes ill."

"A nice situation."

"Has he given you an assignment?"

38

"Executive Officer."

"Thank God for that."

"Why do you say so?"

Vaughn walked to the window and looked out upon the sunlit parade ground. "You've had considerable service, Captain, from your looks and actions. You haven't been here long, but I can tell by your eyes and words how you feel about Fort Joslyn and the garrison here. We're sitting out here on the edge of Apache country, facing hundreds of Mimbrenos and Chiricahuas led by two of the greatest Apache chieftains – Mangus Colorado and Cochise. Cuchillo Rojo keeps us under constant pressure. He's a real bronco, a rim-rock Apache who gets the very breath of life from raiding and killing.

"Major Lester fears Cuchillo Rojo as though he were the very devil himself. I feel sorry for the old man, but it's his responsibilities which bother me more. If Cuchillo Rojo strikes in force, Major Lester will crack up. We have a leavening of Regulars, old veterans, mixed throughout this inadequate command. The rest of the men are green and frightened. As soldiers fighting alone against the Apaches we might have a chance if we were properly led, but we have the civilians here, as well as the responsibility of protecting the people of Santa Theresa."

Vaughn turned. "I'm sorry that you were not allowed to keep on to the Rio Grande, and I wish to God I would have been able to go with you on your journey there, but, as long as you've been ordered to stay here, I'm glad. For you see, Captain, we need a strong hand here if we are to survive."

"It's as bad as all that?"

"You *know* it is, sir."

Travis felt as though he was in a cage with invisible bars – bars composed of the Apache threat and the peremptory orders of an inadequate and frightened old man who was making a poor pretense at commanding a frontier outpost.

"Fort Perilous," said Travis quietly.

Vaughn nodded. "I'll have water brought in for your bath. The tub is in that alcove back there. I'll have your gear brought in, too. The major will expect you at noon mess."

When Vaughn had left, Travis stripped to the buff and swabbed down his sweating body with his filthy shirt. He found a bottle and filled a glass. He dropped on his cot and sipped the strong liquor. In a short time he felt the power of the alcohol seeping through his tired body.

An orderly bustled in with Travis' gear and placed it on a chair. "Is there anything I can do for the captain?" he asked.

"I'll need some water."

"I'll bring it right away, sir."

"Can you have my uniform mended and pressed before noon mess?"

The orderly grinned. "That's one thing we do have here at Joslyn, sir – plenty of seamstresses and washerwomen."

"So I noticed," said Travis dryly.

The orderly eyed the liquor bottle. "Some of the women are right sociable, too, sir."

Travis looked up at the trooper. "Get out of here!"

"Sorry, sir." The orderly flushed as he beat a hasty retreat.

Recall sounded across the post as Travis finished dressing. He buckled on his belt and slid his Colt into the holster. He slapped the dust from his cap and then settled it over one eye. Travis looked at himself in the flyspecked mirror on the wall. He had lost weight on his rough trip to New Mexico. There were hollows in his cheeks, and his nose looked bigger because of the hollows. Somehow his eyes looked harder than usual. Travis took a last drag at his cigar, then threw it into the fireplace. "Here goes," he said aloud.

All of the officers were in the mess with the exception of Major Lester. Clinton Vaughn did the honors. Captain Charles Cass was a

41

big, solidly fleshed man with a sort of ruddy handsomeness, but his eyes were too small to suit Travis. First Lieutenant Kenneth Carlie was a slim-hipped man with broad shoulders. The man's rakish good looks almost concealed the hardness that Travis instinctively felt as soon as he spoke to the officer. Second Lieutenant Martin Newkirk was a mild-looking man who wore spectacles and spoke with an assured polish. Travis placed him as a born gentleman. DeSantis nodded shortly to Travis and then applied himself to a whisky bottle on the sideboard. His face was already a little flushed.

"Attention!" bawled out Captain Cass.

Enos Lester bustled into the mess. "Sit down, gentlemen. You've already met Captain Walker, I'm sure."

There was only small talk during the poor meal. The beef was tough and stringy, and the beans had been cooked too long. The coffee was strong enough to stand a spoon in. DeSantis toyed with his food, and twice during the meal he filled his whisky glass, ignoring the sharp looks of his commanding officer. Enos Lester, for all his talk of ill health, helped himself to three servings, gnawing away at the beef as though his very life depended on it.

When the table had been cleared the orderly

brought out a box of dry cigars and placed a liqueur bottle on the table. Travis looked curiously at the bottle. Lester waved his cigar. "We believe in the amenities here at Fort Joslyn, Captain Walker. No need to go on a Spartan regime merely because we are facing the enemy at our very doorsteps."

"I see," said Travis quietly.

Lester sucked at his cigar. "Now to business," he said. "Captain Walker will relieve Captain Cass as executive officer. Captain Cass will, of course, still remain in command of the infantry section. Mr. Vaughn will remain as quartermaster. Mr. Carlie will command the cavalry section as before, while Mr. DeSantis will act as his second in command, also in charge of the howitzer section. Mr. Newkirk will remain as adjutant."

Charles Cass raised his leonine head. "I would like to know Captain Walker's date of rank."

Travis looked quickly at the man. Their eyes met like thrust and riposte. "April twelfth, eighteen-sixty," said Travis quietly.

Cass flushed.

Enos Lester flicked the ashes from his cigar. "I know my regulations, Captain Cass, sir! I would not have placed Captain Walker as I did without knowing that he ranked you."

Cass nodded, then toyed with his glass. "I hope Captain Walker has plenty of experience in fighting Apaches."

Clinton Vaughn smiled. "He proved that by coming up from the Hatchet Mountains right through Cuchillo Rojo's patrols."

The thin-stemmed liqueur glass snapped in Charles Cass' big hand. DeSantis giggled, and Cass shot him a look of hate. He slowly wiped the blood from his fingers, then filled the fresh glass brought to him by the orderly.

"I'll make a post inspection this afternoon to start off," said Travis.

Enos Lester worked his cigar back and forth in his loose mouth. "Fine! That's the spirit! Perhaps we had better talk about building breastworks between the buildings, for defensive purposes."

DeSantis emptied his glass. "I thought the purpose of cavalry was to attack rather than to defend."

Lester stared at the young officer. "Get thoughts of glory out of your head, Mr. DeSantis. I have a great responsibility here, sir. This post might have to stand a siege."

Cass looked up. "Indians aren't much for siege work," he said.

Martin Newkirk folded his napkin and threaded it through his napkin ring. "We're practically under siege right now, Captain."

44

Lester stood up. "I have no fear of that. Our howitzer section will drive them off in fine shape. Drill those gunners of yours, Mr. DeSantis. Smartly! Smartly!"

The officers stood up. Major Lester relit his cigar. "Now, gentlemen, the affairs of a post commander take up a great deal of time. Come to me with any problems you have. Good afternoon, gentlemen." Lester bustled out.

"The damned old fool," a voice said from the end of the table.

Travis turned to look at Charles Cass. "You're in the presence of junior officers, Captain Cass," he said.

"They know what I mean."

"You'll keep your opinions to yourself."

Cass picked up his cap and placed it on his head. Without a word, he stalked from the mess.

"You've made a great friend there," said Clinton Vaughn.

"A great loss," said Ken Carlie.

Travis looked from one to the other of them. "I want all sections paraded in front of their barracks in one hour. Jump to it, gentlemen."

Later, as Travis walked to his quarters with Clinton Vaughn, he looked out toward the quiet desert. "How much pressure has Cuchillo Rojo put on this place, Clint?"

"Raids. Runs off a horse or mule now and

45

then. Fires into the post at night. Watches the roads to see that we get no reënforcements for supplies. Major Lester sent out two couriers a week ago, twenty-four hours apart. We haven't seen them since."

"You have a civilian scout here?"

"Yes. A man named Baconora."

"From the Mexican town or from the mezcal?"

Clint grinned. "From the mezcal."

"Send him to me."

"Right."

They walked into their quarters. Vaughn filled two glasses. "You have nothing against an after-dinner drink?"

"After that slop I need a good drink."

"Yes."

"Where do you get the cigars and liqueurs?"

"James Morris, the *alcalde* of Santa Theresa, sends them to us now and then."

"An Anglo is *alcalde* of Santa Theresa?"

Clint nodded. "He lived here before the American Occupation and stayed on. The Mexicans love and respect him. He has a great deal of influence in this part of the country."

"He should have abandoned Santa Theresa long before this time."

"You'll learn why he didn't when you meet him."

"I'd like to meet him."

46

"I'm going into Santa Theresa tomorrow to buy supplies. Perhaps you'd like to go along?"

"I will. As long as Major Lester feels responsible for the town, I'll have to see what they can do to help themselves, for it doesn't look to me as though this command can help them too much."

"Amen."

Clint dropped onto his bunk. "Charlie Cass certainly didn't like your taking over exec," he said.

"I'm worried."

"Lester has always been afraid of Charlie Cass. Cass thinks he's quite the soldier. I've heard it said he got his captaincy so quickly because of relatives in Washington. But you know how those stories spread around the latrines."

"What's your personal opinion?"

"I'd rather not say."

"As long as every officer on this post is so damned outspoken about everyone else, you might as well tell me."

"He fancies himself quite a stud. He used to spend a lot of time in the *cantinas* of Santa Theresa until Morris complained to Lester that Cass was bothering Morris' granddaughter Theresa."

"What did Mrs. Cass think about that?"

Clint raised his glass and studied the

47

contents. "That's right," he said, "you haven't yet met Mrs. Cass."

"No."

Clint downed his drink and rolled over to face Travis. "Evelyn Cass is quite a woman. In fact, she's *all* woman, with most of the faults and few of the virtues, but she can still turn the eye of every man on this post except two."

"What two?"

Vaughn grinned. "Charlie, her dearly beloved, and Major Lester. Oh, she's quite the girl, is Evvie."

"Fort Joslyn is quite the place, from what you've been saying."

Vaughn refilled his glass, corked the bottle and tossed it over to Travis. "Fort Joslyn is the rectum of the universe. The cesspool and catchall of the Department of New Mexico. You're the first officer who has been here in months to whom I've been able to talk without hating his guts."

Travis downed his drink and refilled his glass. He corked the bottle and placed it on the table. "You've had quite enough to drink, Clint. Perhaps in a few days you'll classify me with the others."

Vaughn shook his head. "I had resigned myself to this sinkhole, waiting for Cuchillo Rojo to take it over with knife and fire. Now I've suddenly felt that I've received a reprieve." He got up and put on his cap. "I'll send Baconora over to you."

Travis shook his head as the quartermaster left. He emptied his glass, reached for the bottle, then slowly withdrew his hand. It would be too easy to try to find a way out of this stinking mess through the neck of a bottle.

In a few minutes someone tapped on the door. "Come in!" Travis called out.

The door opened, and a man walked in silently. Travis sat up on his cot.

"Baconora," said the man.

"Travis Walker."

"My pleasure, Captain."

Baconora was a man of medium height and build, without a surplus ounce of flesh on his lean body. His eyes were reddish brown, and so was his lank hair. His nose had been smashed by a terrific blow some time in his past. A heavy, tobacco-stained mustache hung down on each side of his thin-lipped mouth. He wore faded and dirty trail clothing, with elaborately carved but worn Mexican boots on his feet. A Navy Colt hung low at his left side for a sidearm draw. It was balanced on the right side by a heavy knife in a wide, fringed sheath.

"Sit down, Baconora," said Travis. "What's the rest of your name?"

"The name is Baconora, sir."

"I see. Drink?"

The scout glanced at the bottle. "Bourbon?"

"Rye."

Baconora shrugged. "It'll do."

"Look in my left saddlebag on the chair there."

The scout drew out Travis' bottle of mezcal. "This is more like it."

Baconora poured a drink and sat down on Vaughn's bunk. "What can I do for you?"

"How bad is this Apache situation?"

"About as bad as it can be."

"How many warriors does Cuchillo Rojo have?"

"*Quién sabe?* Some say a hundred, others say more. Right now he's the big man among the Mimbrenos under Mangus Colorado. Mangus is getting old. Cochise is no spring chicken. The Mimbrenos and Chiricahuas like young leaders like Cuchillo. The young men of both tribes will follow him to hell and back."

"I was afraid of that."

"You know the Apaches?" asked the scout.

"Yes."

"You've fought against them?"

"Mohave-Apaches, Tontos, White Mountain, Chiricahuas, Mimbrenos and Jicarillas."

Baconora grinned crookedly. "You haven't left many of them out."

"I wish I could have at times."

"Hawww! That's good. Hawww!"

The scout downed his drink and refilled his glass. He felt inside his shirt for pipe and tobacco, then filled the pipe. He lit it and leaned back against the wall. "What's on your mind?" he asked.

Travis sat on his chair and tilted it back against the wall. "I've been told two couriers vanished a week or so ago."

The reddish eyes held Travis', and then looked away. "Yeah. Damned fool thing to send them out."

"Why didn't you go?"

"I ain't loco."

"I see. Will you go?"

Baconora shrugged. "What good will it do? Old Lester won't get any reënforcements. From what I've learned the rebels are planning a big buffalo hunt in West Texas."

"So?"

"It ain't no buffalo hunt. Old John R. Baylor is supposed to lead that hunt. He's a colonel in the Provisional Army of the Confederacy. Right now Old John is sitting at Fort Bliss with three or four hundred Texas Mounted Rifles, and they ain't waiting there to hunt buffaloes. They're getting ready to sweep

51

up the Valley of the Rio Grande like a dose of salts and kick the Federals right out of New Mexico."

"You seem to know a lot about the military situation, Baconora."

"I do. That's why it won't do any good for Old Man Lester to try and get reënforcements here from the Rio Grande. We're here, sink or swim, live or die, and all alone, Captain. You can bet your commission on that. Cuchillo Rojo knows that, too. He'll squat out in them hills, watching and waiting, stopping couriers and supply trains at his will. When the time comes he'll take Fort Joslyn and Santa Theresa, too."

A cold feeling crept over Travis. The man was so sure of himself. "Maybe we can do something about that," Travis said quietly.

The scout puffed at his stinking pipe. "Maybe . . . maybe not. You want me to take a pasear into those hills tonight and see what Cuchillo is up to?"

"Can you make it?"

Baconora grinned, revealing even yellow teeth. "I ain't lived in 'Pache country for all these years without being able to get about."

"*Bueno!* Draw anything you need. Report back in three days."

Baconora stood up. He glanced at the bottle.

"Go ahead," said Travis.

"Gracias." Baconora drank deeply and then wiped his mouth with the back of a sleeve. "See you around, captain."

Travis walked to the window and watched the lean scout walk across the parade ground. He passed the troops who were forming for the inspection and headed for the civilian camp at the south end of the post. Travis shrugged. The man must have more than his share of skill and guts to go up into those hills alone.

CHAPTER FOUR

Retreat was over, and the sun was low over the Hatchet Mountains. Travis Walker sat at his desk in headquarters, looking over the results of the afternoon's inspection. The sweat dripped from his face and spattered the inspection sheets. Finally he pushed back the papers and looked at First Sergeant Mack Ellis. "It's a mess," said Travis.

Mack Ellis was a man about as wide as he was high, with hard blue eyes and a mahogany complexion. He had the unmistakable stamp of the old cavalry regular upon him. "The garrison needed new gear and weapons when the war started. Nothing came through from

53

Fort Union. We've had to get by with what we have, sir."

"I appreciate that, Sergeant. But muzzleloading Enfield musketoons for the cavalry! Ye gods! What do they think we're fighting out here? Diggers and Paiutes?"

Mack Ellis shrugged. "Seems as though all the supplies are going to Fort Craig, sir, where the department commander is concentrating regulars, volunteers and militia to stop the threatened rebel advance up the Valley of the Rio Grande."

"Wouldn't it be just fine if the rebels swung west to strike into Arizona and found just us at Fort Joslyn to stop them?"

"For this we are soldiers, Captain."

Travis nodded. "By Act of Congress, out of Necessity."

Ellis grinned. "Forgotten by our sires and mistreated by our mothers."

"How are the horses?"

"Not too good. We had fine mounts up until a month or so ago. Then we lost all of them and had to get second-rate remounts."

"How were they lost?"

"Epidemic glanders, sir. We lost forty-five mounts. Had to shoot most of them. Had to destroy the old stables."

"I see. Just another bead in the necklace of unfortunate circumstances."

"The captain has a fine way of putting things."

Travis smashed a hand down on the desk. "Those blasted musketoons are too muzzle-heavy. I want you to have your ordnance artificer remove the butt plates and drill a hole in the butt stock large enough to take about eight ounces of lead. That should make the difference."

There was a look of admiration in Ellis' eyes. "I should have thought of that, Captain."

Travis stood up. "Have him work on two or three at a time. We can't take chances on men unarmed."

"I'll see to it right away, sir."

Travis wiped the sweat from his face. Major Lester was taking his siesta, which Travis had been told took place between Retreat and evening mess. The old man, despite his fears, made sure nothing disturbed the routine of forty years' service.

"I want target practice tomorrow morning, Sergeant," said Travis over his shoulder, "each man to fire twenty rounds with the weapon he is armed with. The infantry will fire the first relays, which should allow enough time for the ordnance artificer to have the musketoons weighted and ready for the mounted troops to fire in the afternoon. Do you have butts set up?"

"There is a low ridge to the west of the fort which will serve the purpose."

"Good! Officers, not noncommissioned officers, will be in charge of the firing of their respective units. When each unit is through firing they will prepare enough cartridges to replace those they have expended. Quartermaster Vaughn tells me there is enough cartridge paper, bar lead and powder for the purpose. It might be best if the troops expended their older cartridges in order that they have fresh rounds in case of an attack."

"Yes, sir."

"Jump to it then."

It was dusk when Travis left headquarters and stood outside beneath the ramada to get a breath of fresh air. The mingled odors of cooking beef and beans hung over the post in the windless air. Travis walked toward his quarters and was even with a low adobe fronted by a ramada when he suddenly became aware of a woman standing beneath the ramada.

Travis turned to look at her. She came to the front of the ramada and placed a hand against one of the posts. "Captain Walker?" she asked in a low voice.

"Yes."

"I am Evelyn Cass. I haven't had the pleasure of meeting you."

Travis eyed her. She was fairly tall and very well formed. Her dark hair was parted in the middle and drawn back into a large cluster at the nape of her shapely neck. A fine Mexican comb had been thrust through the cluster. Her skin had not been exposed to the blazing suns of New Mexico, and even in the dimness Travis could see that it was milky white. Her eyes were exceptionally large and set wide apart. Her mouth drew Travis' attention. It was wide and full-lipped, with a sensuous quality about it.

Travis took off his forage cap and bowed. "A pleasure to make your acquaintance, Mrs. Cass."

She came forward. "I stay in the quarters to avoid the heat of the day," she said. "I love the starlit nights of New Mexico."

The faint odor of jasmine came to Travis. She wore a clinging gown which revealed her full breasts and hips. "Charles has spoken of you," she said.

"I am honored."

There was a subtle look in her dark eyes. "You are the first new officer we have had here in quite some time. One gets tired of the same faces and worn-out conversations. You must

57

honor us by having dinner with us."

"I'd appreciate it, Mrs. Cass."

She looked him up and down. "You've had some interesting adventures getting here," she said.

"More dangerous than interesting, I'm afraid."

She pressed her body back against one of the ramada posts and hooked her hands together behind it. It had the effect of extending her full breasts toward Travis. "Do you expect to go on to the Rio Grande?"

He smiled ruefully. "I had intended to, but Major Lester stopped that."

"I hope we all may leave soon. I had hopes Charles would be assigned to the staff at Santa Fe. It's so gay there."

"It might not be if the rebels advance up the Valley."

She shrugged. "Anything would be better than being penned here at Fort Joslyn. *Fort Joslyn* . . . it isn't anything but a run-down outpost."

Boots thudded against the hard caliche of the parade ground and the tall figure of Charles Cass appeared. He stopped short as he saw them. Evelyn Cass smiled. "I have been passing the time of day with Captain Walker, Charles," she said.

"So I see."

"You didn't find time to introduce me so I introduced myself."

Cass nodded. He looked at Travis. "What's this about target practice tomorrow?"

"The orders will be posted this evening?"

"It's a waste of time."

"When was the last time you had practice?"

Cass waved a big hand. "Some months ago. If the Apaches hear us firing they'll get excited. You might have an attack on the men firing."

"Then they'll get some real practice, won't they, Captain?"

Cass flushed. "We haven't too many cartridges."

"There are plenty of materials to make more."

"The major might not think so."

"Then he can stop the practice."

Cass drew in his broad chin and bent his head forward. His big hands half closed, then opened again. He looked almost as though he meant to rush Travis.

"Dinner is on the table, Charles," said Evelyn Cass quickly.

Charles nodded. But he kept his eyes on Travis.

Travis bowed to Evelyn. "Good evening, Mrs. Cass," he said. He walked a few feet and then turned to look at Cass. "I'm riding into Santa Theresa in the morning," he said. "You'll take over in my place until I return."

"I've got plenty work of my own to do, Captain Walker."

Travis smiled thinly. "I've already given my orders – all you have to do is make sure they're carried out." He walked away.

"Damn him!" grated Charles Cass.

Evelyn Cass laughed. "Just look at you! He certainly slipped the bit into your mouth, Charles."

He gripped her by the arm and pushed her ahead of him into the dark interior of their quarters. "You're hurting me," she said.

He shoved her back against the wall and slapped her face so that her head snapped back against the plastered above. "Don't ever laugh at me like that again!" he snarled.

She touched her bruised mouth and looked at him with hate in her big eyes. "You never could stand to be laughed at."

"In any case *you* won't laugh at me."

Her right hand dropped to her side and gripped a bottle which stood on the table beside her. "And you won't strike me again," she said coldly.

He stood there and stared at her, then turned on a heel and walked away. "I'll put Travis Walker in his place. You'll see."

She released the bottle and a cynical smile

curved her bleeding lips. She had been looking for a long time to find a way to get rid of Charles Cass and leave Fort Joslyn. She knew now, if she played her cards right, she might make it. She also knew she had the right cards to play. She stroked her full body with her slim hands.

Travis Walker lay on his cot, stripped to his drawers, feeling the cool fingers of the night breeze touch his hot body. Evelyn Cass was quite a woman, especially to a man penned up on a two-bit post like Fort Joslyn. Travis had been thinking of her ever since he had talked with her. Clint Vaughn had said she was quite a woman, with most of the faults and few of the virtues of her sex. He had also said she could still turn the eye of every man except two on the post – Charlie Cass and Enos Lester. Clint had been exactly correct when he had made his statement.

Travis stood up and walked to the window that looked out on the parade ground. Faint moonlight gave the parade ground a silvery hue. The reflection of flames from a big fire down at the civilian camp danced on the walls of the farrier shop. The civilians had been making a lot of noise ever since the evening meal. Now and then the shrill laughter of a woman broke out over the low voices of the men. Bottles were being passed around. It had been in Clint's mind to ask Major Lester to stop the civilians from drinking too much, but, as Clint had told Travis, the major had refused to do so. The result was a nightly drinking party, and more than once in the past week there had been several bloody fights among the men and some skirmishing among the women.

The major had given orders that the soldiers were not to mingle with the civilians during these affairs, but it wasn't easy to stop them. Several times the guard had turned troopers and women out of the hay piles behind the long stables.

Clint Vaughn came across the parade ground. He stopped to look at the big fire, then shrugged and came on toward the quarters. He came into the dark room.

"Some racket down there," said Travis over his shoulder.

Clint scaled his hat at a peg and then stripped off gun belt and shirt. "The major seems to think it keeps up their morale."

"It doesn't help the morale of the garrison."

Clint dropped onto his bunk. "No."

"Who is officer of the guard tonight?"

"DeSantis."

"Well, he'd better have them quiet down before Taps or he'll answer to me."

Clint lay back on his bunk. "Drink?"

"No."

"I agree. It just seems to make you heat up more."

Travis sat down and tilted the chair back against the wall to feel the cross draft of air against his body. "You were told about firing practice tomorrow?"

"Yes. Corporal Covello will issue cartridge paper, lead and powder for fresh cartridges. Sergeant Hoeffle will have bullet moulds ready."

"What time do we leave tomorrow?"

"Early. The major didn't object?"

"No. He was eager to have me go."

"It'll be a big change for me, not that Santa Theresa has much to offer in the way of amusement other than strong liquor and loose women."

"That should add up to something."

"Wait until you taste the liquor and see the women."

"I met Evelyn Cass this evening."

"So?"

"You analyzed her quite well."

Clint laughed. "I've been looking at her with more than the eyes of friendship for some time."

"Cass wasn't too happy about the firing tomorrow."

"He might have to stay out in the sun for a while. He's putting on weight, and he suffers from the heat quite a bit."

"He'll suffer a hell of a lot more from the heat in hell if we don't have target practice."

Clint nodded. "Charlie is lazy. He'll do anything to get out of exerting himself, with a few exceptions."

"Such as?"

"Lifting a schooner of beer and having a tumble in bed with any woman he can get to lie with him."

"With the wife he has?"

Clint raised himself on an elbow. "In my opinion, they hate each other's guts. I'll bet they have some good go-arounds when they're alone, and I don't mean it the way you're thinking right now."

Travis pulled on his trousers and then his boots.

"Where are you going?" asked Clint.

"Out for some air."

"Stay within the post quadrangle."

Travis shrugged into his shirt and buckled his gun belt about his slim waist. "I know better than to go beyond the post at night. How close in do the Mimbrenos come?"

Clint held his hands about two inches apart. "You'll hear them talking to each other out there."

Travis picked up his cap and put it on his head. He drew his Colt and twirled the cylinder to see that each nipple was capped. "See you," he said.

There were only two lights showing on the post, a lamp in the guardhouse and the bright fire of the civilians. Travis walked to the gate and stood beside the sentry. "How is it tonight?" asked Travis.

The sentry shrugged. "You can hear the Mimbrenos out there once in a while. If it wasn't for all that noise at the fire we'd be able to hear the Apaches better, sir."

"Step back behind the buttress of the building, soldier. You're silhouetted against that fire."

The sentry nodded and moved behind the buttress. Travis turned. If anyone walked between the fire and the darkness of the desert he'd be a fair shot for an Apache marksman.

"Listen," said the sentry.

A night bird had called not fifty yards beyond the gate. A moment later another bird answered the first a hundred yards to the west.

"It's them," said the sentry.

Suddenly a coyote's shrieking laugh split the momentary quiet, then died away. The wind shifted a little and carried the melancholy howling of another coyote from a low ridge west of the fort.

"Fair gives a man the shivers, sir," said the sentry.

Travis nodded. He had never quite got used to the cry of a coyote as imitated by an Indian, while, on the contrary, he had always sensed a melancholy sort of enjoyment from the true cry of the scavenging animals.

A woman laughed near the fire. A bottle smashed. Travis cut swiftly across the gap of the gate to the next building and walked down the west side of the quadrangle. Fifty feet from the fire he walked between two buildings and stood in the dimness of a building ell to look west. Then he saw what he was looking for. The firelight had glistened for a fraction of a second on something moist out there – something like a bright amber bead.

Travis drew in his breath. The Mimbreno was no more than fifty yards from the closest building.

Travis walked back to the quadrangle, toward the fire. A trooper stood up and scuttled for cover. Two men and three women sat by the fire. One of them was Ben Joad. Travis scooped up a bucketful of foul-smelling water from a fire barrel placed at one corner of the quartermaster warehouse. He walked quickly to the fire and cast the water over it.

"What the hell!" roared Joad as he leaped to

66

his feet. His trousers had been soaked. Steam rose from the fire.

Maggie Gillis giggled. "It's the good-lookin' officer who just come in."

"I'll fix his good looks!" snarled Joad. He whipped his hand back for his knife. The other man staggered drunkenly in between Joad and Travis. Travis drew his Colt and slapped the heavy octagonal barrel against the drunk's head, driving him down to his knees. The woman beside Maggie Gillis screamed.

"Corporal of the guard! Post Number Four!" yelled a sentry.

Joad kicked the drunk flat, then came at Travis with his knife lying flat in his right hand, at waist level. Travis jumped back and stumbled over a bottle. The knife tip slashed through his left sleeve, and he winced as the metal sliced into his forearm.

"I'll teach yuh, brassbounder!" yelled Joad.

The woman who had screamed snatched up the bucket Travis had dropped and swung it in a wild arc toward Travis' head, but Maggie Gillis was too quick. She stepped forward and fended the bucket off with her left forearm. Then she drove in a hard right jab that connected neatly with the enraged woman's jaw and sprawled her backward over the prostrate drunk, with a wild show of dirty petticoats.

Joad closed in as he heard the tramping of feet as the guard approached the south end of the fort. He thrust in at Travis with the knife. Travis leaped sideways, switching the Colt from his right hand to his left. He gripped Joad's right wrist and pulled him off balance at the same time. Travis struck swiftly at the base of the civilian's neck with the barrel of the six-shooter. Joad fell downward into the hot ashes of the fire and lay still. Travis gripped Joad by his ankles and dragged him from the ashes. He hooked a boot under the man and rolled him over.

The guard stopped behind Travis. "Jesus, lookit," said a trooper. He pointed at Joad's ash-smeared face. Joad's short beard was smoldering, and the embers beneath the bed of ashes had seared the left side of his face.

Travis holstered his Colt. As he did so he heard the sound of a shot west of the post. The slug struck a trooper with the sound of a stick being whipped into thick mud. The trooper folded over, dropping his musketoon with a clatter. "Scatter!" roared Travis.

They scattered behind buildings and wagons. There was silence for a few moments, then suddenly a demoniac cry came from the darkness west of the post. It was diabolical, more like an animal's cry than a man's. The blood curdling cry came again, then died away. Then, faintly, the sound of hoofbeats came from the sandy ridges to the west.

Travis knelt by the shot trooper and rolled him over. Sightless eyes stared up at him. Travis wiped the blood from his hands and stood up. "Corporal," he called out. "Throw Joad and those other two into the guard-house. Have the medical orderly dress Joad's face and examine the other two." He looked for Maggie Gillis. She was leaning against a wagon, holding her left forearm. Travis walked to her. "Are you hurt?" he asked quietly.

She laughed. "Just a bruise. How's your arm?"

He took his bandanna from his neck and bound it about the slash. "I'll be all right. You've got quite a wallop in that right hand, Miss Gillis."

"Maggie!"

"All right . . . Maggie then. That bucket might have cracked my skull."

She shrugged. "I like a fair fight," she said. She looked up at him. "You've marked Ben Joad for life, Captain. He won't never forget it. You look out for him."

"Thanks. I will."

She brushed back a strand of her straggling hair. "You sure got a direct way about you."

He smiled. "It works."

"It'll keep on working if you live long enough to talk about it."

The guard carried the trooper off. Travis watched them. "A good man died tonight because of the foolishness here."

"What will you do with Ben and the others?"

"Ben can sit in the guardhouse a day or two. When the others are sober they will be freed. What is Ben to you, Maggie?"

She straightened up and thrust out her chin. "Not a damned thing, and don't you forget it!"

He shrugged as she walked away into the darkness.

Maggie walked to her quarters. A trooper sidled up out of the darkness. "How about messing around tonight, Mag?" he asked.

"Get out of here, Scully."

He gripped her by the arm and whirled her about. Maggie timed it perfectly. Her open right hand smacked loudly against his face. "I told you to get out of here!" she cried.

Scully watched her walk into her quarters. He felt his stinging face. "Now I wonder what's got into her?" he asked aloud.

Travis walked over to the guardhouse. "Where's Mr. DeSantis?" he asked a trooper.

The trooper pointed to DeSantis' quarters.

"He's been in there for some time."

Travis crossed the parade ground to DeSantis' quarters. He opened the door and walked in. He could see two men asleep on their cots in the dimness. One of them sat up. "Who is it?" he asked.

"Walker, Newkirk."

Travis gripped DeSantis by the shoulder and shook him. DeSantis sat up. "What the hell is this?" he asked.

"You're officer of the guard. What are you doing in bed?"

DeSantis slid his legs out from beneath the covers. "I told the sergeant of the guard to awaken me at midnight for my rounds."

"Get into your uniform and double-time down to the guardhouse. Didn't you hear the noise out there?"

The young officer shook his head.

Travis stepped back and hooked his thumbs over his gun belt. "The mesquite is thick with Apaches. Ben Joad and his cronies had a hell of a fire going, and they were making enough noise to awaken the dead. Joad came after me with a knife. One of the members of the guard was killed by a sharpshooting buck. You were supposed to be alert, mister. Now get out there and keep up your rounds all night. Every hour on the hour! I want no fires and no noise!"

71

DeSantis dressed hurriedly. Newkirk lit a lamp. His serious face studied Travis. "I've been expecting something like this," he said quietly. "You should have stayed at the guard-house as I suggested, Norval."

"Shut up, you pen pusher!"

Newkirk flushed. DeSantis buckled his gun belt and hooked his saber to it. He jammed his hat onto his head and stamped from the room.

Martin Newkirk shook his head. "We've been sloppy here, Captain Walker. Too sloppy. I'm glad you're here to tighten up this post."

"I can't say that I am."

The young lieutenant stood up. "I've been afraid of what might happen here, sir. But with you as executive officer I'm sure we are at least strengthened against our main enemies."

"I didn't have much choice in the matter, Newkirk. My orders were superseded by those of Major Lester's. My duty is here now, and I'm going to see to it that it is done to the best of my ability."

"I'm sure it will be. You said, sir, that Major Lester's orders superseded yours. May I ask how?"

"Simple enough. I was ordered to report to the commanding officer of the department when I had completed my mission in Arizona. I arrived here to learn that, since then, other orders had been issued, holding me here."

"Specifically, sir?"

Travis looked quickly at the serious-faced young soldier. "What do you mean, mister?"

"Did the orders *name* you?"

"No. It was a so-called blanket order."

Newkirk nodded. "I thought so."

"What are you driving at, mister?"

"I assume your orders were important to the defense of the Southwest by the United States Army. I cannot fathom why Major Lester would force you to to remain here knowing how important your mission was."

"I saw and read the order stating that all officers and men, who had no definite assignment and were separated from their commands, would report to the nearest camp, post or station of the United States Army for such duty as would be prescribed by the commanding officer of any such camp, post or station, until orders were received from the department commander ordering them elsewhere." Travis smiled. "And so on and so on."

Newkirk nodded. "I know the usual verbiage. Major Lester, if you'll pardon me for saying so, is a very frightened old man who has developed imaginary ills to cover up his fright. He needs you, but you are really more valuable elsewhere."

Travis shrugged. "I'm here now and here I'll stay, because if I don't I'll be put under arrest by Major Lester. Good night, Mr. Newkirk." Travis left the quarters.

Martin Newkirk walked to the window and watched Travis stride off. "Odd," he said quietly. "Very odd indeed."

CHAPTER FIVE

Clinton Vaughn drew in his horse and felt inside his shell jacket for his cigar case. He looked at Travis Walker. "Let's give the horses a breather."

Travis slanted his hat low over his eyes and looked at the salmon-colored hills. The mesquite and sage stippled them like cloves in a ham. There wasn't a breath of air moving across the baking desert. Far across the dun sands a wind devil rose to towering height and swept toward the hills in a wild, whirling dance.

Clint passed a cigar to Travis. "The town is beyond those hills."

Travis lit up. "I wonder why those people didn't leave? Some parts of Arizona are practically deserted. Once thriving communities are now ghost towns."

"You haven't yet met James Morris, the *alcalde*."

"He must be quite a man to keep these people here."

Clint lit his cigar and blew out a puff of bluish smoke. "James Morris is practically a legend around this part of the country. Mexicans and Anglos look up to him as though he was the prophet Moses."

"Wandering in the wilderness."

Clint nodded. "It's too late for them to leave now. There are no United States troops between here and the Colorado to protect them if they move that way. North there are nothing but mountains and deserted towns. South into Mexico is a wilderness of burned ranches and deserted *placitas*. The Apaches are hammering on the gates of Durango. Between here and the Rio Grande there is nothing but painted death for travelers."

Travis nodded. Suddenly he took the cigar from his mouth. "There seems to be a little painted death near here right now."

A puff of smoke had shot up from a hill not more than two miles away from them. It was quickly followed by two more.

Clinton Vaughn swallowed. "We'd better get on into Santa Theresa," he said quickly. "I feel as though I suddenly need a drink –

75

two, in fact."

They rode swiftly on toward Santa Theresa. There was a place where low sand ridges closed in on the rutted road, and they kept their eyes on the brushy slopes, riding with carbines loaded and cocked across their thighs.

Smoke drifted up ahead of them. Travis drew in his sorrel a little, but Clint waved him on. "The town," he said.

Santa Theresa seemed to sleep in the sun on a wide stretch of sand. Trees showed the course of a stream. Wisps of smoke rose from chimneys. On a hill behind the town the mine workings could be seen, but there seemed to be no activity about the workings. The town itself was typical of that part of the country. The adobes and jacals formed a square about a dusty littered plaza. Pigs, chickens, dogs and cats scattered from in front of the two cantering horses as Travis and Clint reached the edge of the plaza. The adobes were well and solidly built, but some of them were badly in need of plastering. Vegetation had sprouted on some of the sagging roofs. Doors and windows were tightly closed, and there was a brooding air about the little town.

Across the plaza Travis saw a two-storied *torreon*, or defensive tower, obviously built generations ago as protection against marauding Apaches. There were great cracks in the round tower. Other than the little church, the only building in the whole assembly that looked as though it had been taken care of was a low rambling structure situated on a low knoll at the west side of the plaza. The doors had been freshly painted in pale blue, while the shutters were faint pink. Ollas hung from the ramada beams, and bright flowers cascaded from the ollas.

"That's the *alcalde's* house," said Clint, pointing to the low building with his cigar. "Old man Morris keeps it looking nice. The rest of the people here just don't give a damn since the Apache threat. They just sit around and brood, waiting for something to happen, and, by God, if they don't get out of here one way or another something disastrous *will* happen."

They swung down from their horses in front of a yellow-painted *cantina*. Great scabrous flakes of plaster and paint littered the ground along the walls. The door sagged on its great leather hinges.

"The house of Jonas Simpson," said Clint. "The place stinks, but not as badly as some of the Mex *cantinas*. Come on, I'll buy you a drink."

They walked into the dim interior. Half a dozen men sat at tables, drinking and playing monte. "Here comes the sojer boys," said a man with an English accent.

" 'Bout time they did somethin' about them 'Paches," said a little man who was half concealed under a battered Mexican steeple hat encrusted with coin-silver filigree work. Despite the heat of the day, he wore a gay but filthy-looking serape over his narrow shoulders.

"Shut up, Vince!" roared a man from behind the bar.

Flies buzzed up from the liquor slopped on the zinc-topped bar as Clint and Travis stopped in front of it. A huge man stood behind the bar, mopping it with a filthy rag. His bald head glistened with droplets of sweat. A bright blue eye surveyed Travis from the right socket; the left eye was long gone, leaving a puckered, evil-looking hole.

"Mr. Jonas Simpson," Clinton Vaughn said to Travis with an air, as though he was introducing royalty. "Captain Travis Walker, new executive officer at Fort Joslyn."

Simpson extended a thick arm from which depended a massive paw of a hand. He gripped Travis' hand. "Pleased, I'm sure," he rumbled. "What's your pleasure, gents? On the house."

"*Aguardiente*," said Travis.

"The same, mine host," said Clint.

Vince called out, "That include us, Jonas?"

"You ain't paid me for the last three drinks you had, Vince," Jonas said sourly.

Vince cackled. "What the hell difference does it make? The 'Paches will soon take over, Jonas."

Jonas picked up an empty bottle and hurled it across the room. It smashed just over Vince's head, splattering him with glass. "Get out, you buzzard!" yelled Jonas.

Vince grinned. He threw down his cards, brushed the glass from serape and hat brim and stood up, sweeping the hat from his head and bowing low, then sauntering to the door. "I'll take my business elsewhere," he said over his shoulder.

"Good riddance," said Jonas. He placed a bottle and two glasses before the two officers.

"How does it go?" asked Clint.

"Rotten," said the *cantina* keeper. "Oh, there's enough drinking, more than usual if the truth be known, but most of it is jawbone. No work around here. No pay. So it goes. I carry these chiselers on jawbone and I ain't so sure old Cuchillo Rojo won't wipe out them tabs when he makes up his mind to take the town – and the fort too, if the truth be known."

"Now, Jonas," chided Clint as he filled the glasses.

"Well, it's plain as the nose on your face, Mr. Vaughn."

"Maybe so."

"You know it is!"

Clint grinned. He looked at Travis. "Jonas is the fount of all gossip in Santa Theresa. The oracle of this part of New Mexico. An old soldier, scarred by honorable wounds."

Jonas placed a hand across his gaping eye socket. "Lost it at Chapultepec under Old Rough and Ready – General Zachary Taylor, God rest his soul."

Travis looked quickly at Jonas and then at Clint. Clint kicked Travis' right ankle. The quartermaster downed his drink and refilled his glass. "How is the old man?" he asked.

Jonas shook his head. "Somehow he just doesn't seem to understand how bad it really is. Says he's weathered many an Apache scare hereabouts."

"We didn't see any guards about the town."

"Yeh, 'cause they're all sitting in *cantinas* swilling rot gut. Cuchillo could go through here like a dose of salts if he had a mind to."

"The *torreon* was supposed to be repaired."

Jonas laughed without humor. "That damned old wreck? We'd be better off if we tore it down and built a new one, but there ain't anyone around here who'll sweat out in that sun to do it."

"So what is Morris doing?"

Jonas shrugged. "Sitting in his chair with his cane of office across his lap, listening to the poor, sick and needy like he always does. Now and then he calls a meeting of the head men of the town and talks about cleaning out the well, painting the 'dobes, keeping the animals off the plaza grass."

"What grass?"

Jonas tilted his head to one side. "He still thinks we have grass." He took a drink himself. "Sometimes I can talk some of the boys into standing guard at evening and at dawn when there ain't no sun. The rest of the time they sit around and drink. *Jesusita!*"

Travis emptied his glass and waved Jonas' hand back as he started to refill the glass. "We're going to see the *alcalde*," he said.

Jonas filled the glass. "Then you'll need this, Captain."

Clint nodded. They finished their drinks and walked outside. "Come back after you're done!" roared Jonas.

"Quite a character," said Travis. "Wounded at Chapultepec with Old Rough and Ready, eh? Quite a feat that. Considering Zach Taylor was never there."

Clint grinned. "Lost his eye in a barroom

81

brawl in Mesilla, but he likes to talk about being at Chapultepec. We all have our little lies, Travis."

"Yes. He doesn't seem too happy about conditions here. Are they as bad as he says?"

"Probably worse. I'm afraid James Morris lives pretty much in the past."

They led their mounts over to the *alcalde's* house. "Nice place," observed Travis.

Clint tethered his horse to the rail. "The old man has been here for a long time. He's a fixture here. Made his money in trading. Used to take *conductas* of trading goods down into Chihuahua and sometimes beyond. He's a man who had position and wealth back in the States but forsook all of it to come out here when he was a young man. He's almost more of a Mexican than he is an Anglo. He has two loves left in his life."

"Two – at *his* age?"

"I meant his granddaughter Theresa and the town here. She was named after the patron saint of the town. She is the issue of the old man's only son Theodore and a Mexican woman who was probably part Indian. When you see Theresa you'll know what I mean."

A shout echoed throughout the plaza. They turned to see two men tumble out of an open doorway and roll over and over in the dust, biting, kicking and clawing at each other. Half a dozen men came out to watch the brawl. A slatternly woman whose brown breasts hung half over the top of a ragged gown came out to join them. "Gut him, Frank!" she screamed.

Doors opened and people came out to watch the cursing, sweating combatants. One of the men got to his feet. The other man started to get up, but a boot connected against his jaw, the cruel Mexican spur roweling his bearded face. The droplets of bright blood splattered the caliche beneath him. Once again the tall man booted his vanquished opponent.

The woman ran to the tall man and drew a knife from her bosom. She thrust it toward the man. "Go on!" she screamed. "Gut him. The pig called me a *puta!*"

The tall man shoved her back, wiped a bloody nose and staggered into the *cantina* followed by the other man, who slapped him on the back. The woman hurled the knife at the door.

"Nice town," said Travis dryly. "Reminds me of last night at the post."

"There really isn't any law here. Morris does what he can. Now and then he calls for soldiers from Joslyn, but lately Major Lester has refused him."

Travis walked up onto the warped wooden porch. Between Fort Joslyn and Santa Theresa he would have his hands more than full. The

83

lonely feeling swept over him again. The whole country was girding for war. North and South getting ready for a bloody fracas, while he was standing on the edge of a gulf in western New Mexico – a gulf of hate, peopled by the tigers of the human species, the Apaches. There was no one to pull him back from that gulf nor anyone to catch him if he fell.

Clinton Vaughn hammered on the great bolt-studded door of the *casa*. "This is probably the only house in Santa Theresa that could stand any kind of siege," he said over his shoulder.

Travis nodded. The walls were thick. He could see that by the deepness of the door embrasure. The roof supports that extended from the upper front wall just beneath the thatched ramada were of great size, and they had been carved by some crude sculptor. The shade of the ramada was a relief after the blazing heat of the morning sun. The shutters were thick and in good condition, and Travis figured that they and the doors must have sheet iron sandwiched in between layers of thick wood to hold back arrows and bullets. James Morris had built well.

"It is Lieutenant Vaughn from Fort Joslyn, with Captain Travis Walker."

"*Sí! Sí!* The smiling lieutenant!"

The great door creaked open, and a flood of cool air poured about the two sweating officers. A dumpy Mexican woman ushered them in: "You're getting prettier every day, Angelique," said Clint. "Be careful. I'm looking for a woman to clean up my quarters and make me happy."

Angelique tittered. She flapped her apron up and down. "I cannot leave the *alcalde*," she said.

Clint shrugged sorrowfully. "I thought as much. Well, he is a fine looking man with many *pesos*. I do not have a chance with the pretty *señoritas* with him around."

Travis shook his head. Angelique closed and bolted the huge door, then led the way up a tiled corridor. The walls were hung with Indian and Mexican blankets.

Angelique opened a massive door at the end of the corridor and ushered Travis and Clint in. They entered a large, low-ceilinged room. The windows were sealed by shutters, and the room was lit by sweet-smelling candles held in large silver candelabra. The candlelight reflected from the white-washed walls of the room and from the polished wood of the heavy furniture. A small candle in a red glass guttered before a carved wooden *santo* placed in a deep wall-niche.

A tall man sat in a great carved chair. His

lower limbs were swathed in a thick Navajo blanket. His strong gnarled hands clasped a silver-knobbed ebony cane which lay across his thighs. His face was long and strong, with a well-trimmed mustache and short white beard. A shock of thick white hair was carefully brushed. It was his eyes that held Travis' attention. They were light blue, steady and thoughtful, and they seemed to reveal the deep inner peace of the old man.

"*Buenos dias, señor, alcalde,*" said Clint.

"*Buenos dias, Teniente Vaughn,*" answered the old man.

"*Como ha estado?*"

The *alcalde* waved a hand. "*Regular; lo mismo.*"

"*Tengo el gusto de presentarle al Captain Travis Walker.*"

The old man extended a hand. "*Gusto en conocerle, Captain Walker.*"

Travis gripped the proffered hand and was surprised at the powerful grip of the old man. "My pleasure, sir," he said.

"Do you speak Spanish, Captain?"

Travis smiled. "*Más o meno, señor alcalde.*"

"If you prefer, sir, we will speak in English."

"I would prefer it, sir. My Spanish is of the cow-pen variety."

The old man smiled gently. "I speak it
86

almost as much as I do English. It is a beautiful language that sometimes lends itself to nuances which are not quite the same in English. You must understand I have spent many years with my adopted people here in the Southwest."

"I understand, sir."

"My house is your, *señor capitán.* Do sit down."

Travis and Clint drew up chairs before the old man. James Morris reached to the table and tinkled a small bell. Angelique appeared almost instantly. "We will have wine, Angelique," said James Morris.

"Yes, *señor mayor.*"

James Morris smiled at Travis. "You are new here in our country, are you not?"

"I have just arrived. I will serve at Fort Joslyn for a time."

"That is good. You must come and have dinner with me. You are from the States?"

"No. From Fort Yuma on the Colorado."

"I see. How are conditions there?"

"Fort Yuma is strongly held by a good garrison. I wish I could say the same about the rest of the Southwest."

"These are hard times. Brother against brother and father against son."

Clinton Vaughn leaned forward. "The

captain has come with me to talk about the protection of Santa Theresa."

"We will take care of ourselves. We have strong men here, well armed, who do not fear the Apache."

Travis leaned back in his chair. The old man was living in a fool's paradise, from what Travis had seen both at Fort Joslyn and Santa Theresa.

"The mines are not being worked," said Clint, "nor is there any trading going on."

James Morris smiled. "We have lived through bad times and good. In the language of my adopted people – *'No hay mal que por no bien venga!'* "

Travis looked at Clint. Clint shrugged and held out his hands, palms upward. Travis shot an angry glance at Clint. His action was rude beyond belief. The old man had said that there is no evil which may not be turned into good. But James Morris seemed to be unaffected by Clint's rude gesture.

Clint felt for a cigar. He took one out and handed it to Travis. Then he leaned forward and handed one to James Morris. The old man placed it in his mouth, drew out a lucifer and lit the cigar. "I do not often get the cigars," he said with satisfaction. "Theresa seems to think they affect my health."

Travis and Clint lit up. Travis eyed the old

man. There was something odd about James Morris, but he could not put his finger on it.

Angelique bustled in and placed a bottle and three glasses upon the table. James Morris reached for the bottle and took out the cork. He filled the three glasses. "Help yourselves, gentlemen," he said.

Travis took his glass and sipped the wine. It seemed to have the sun and wind in it, the smell of the sage and the warmth of the Southwestern sun, in a subtle sort of a way. He put his glass on the table. "Mr. Morris," he said, "Major Lester has appointed me his executive officer, and because of that I have come here to Santa Theresa to investigate conditions. I find here an undefended town with people drinking during the day and morale at a very low ebb. The hills are thick with Apaches, just waiting for a chance to strike against your *placita*.

"The garrison at Fort Joslyn is small, but part of our responsibility is the safety of Santa Theresa."

James Morris raised a hand as though in protest. *"Las aparencias enganan."*

Travis felt a surge of anger within him. "I *know* appearances are deceptive, but the fact remains that you are here in a practically undefended town. You have no reliable defenses, *señor mayor.*"

"We have the *torreon*. It has done us good services in past years."

"This is a brutal question, Mayor Morris, but have you seen your *torreon* lately?"

James Morris swung out his ebony cane and thudded its tip against the tiled floor. "I have no need to do so! My people know their responsibilities as laid down by their mayor! Some weeks ago I ordered them to reënforce that tower; I feel sure they have done so."

Travis ignored a quick gesture by Clinton Vaughn. "The fact is this, *señor mayor* – the *torreon* has *not* been repaired. There *are* no guards watching those hills. The garrison at Fort Joslyn is hardly able to take care of itself."

Clint shot an angry glance at Travis. Travis waved a hand at him. "I would like an estimate of the situation from you, *señor mayor*."

James Morris' big hands clenched and then relaxed. "Who *is* this man, Lieutenant Vaughn?"

Clinton Vaughn emptied his glass. "The man who is probably capable of saving all of us, *señor mayor*."

"I am not accustomed to be bearded in such a manner, Lieutenant Vaughn."

Clint shrugged. "The very esteemed Captain Walker may be speaking the truth, *señor mayor*."

The *alcalde* gripped his cane. "This man you have brought here is a *Yanqui!*"

Clinton Vaughn shrugged in an elaborate gesture. "Yes, *mi mayor,* but he speaks the truth."

The door swung open and a young woman entered the room. She closed the door behind her. Travis turned to look fully at her, and his breath caught in his throat. She was little more than twenty years of age, but her figure was that of a perfectly developed woman. "Are you all right, Grandfather?" she asked in a soft voice that was slightly accented.

Travis could not take his eyes from her. She seemed to be an amalgamation of the better qualities of Anglo Mexican and Indian; her face had a cameolike beauty which would catch and hold any man's attention, be he hot-blooded young buck or almost senile oldster. She was woman in the very essence of the word, with all the good and bad that is woman itself in her expression. She walked to her grandfather and slid a smooth arm about his wrinkled neck. Travis was fascinated by her and it took a hidden kick from Clinton Vaughn for Travis to remember his manners. He stood up.

"This is my granddaughter, Captain Walker," said James Morris with quiet pride.

Theresa Morris extended a slim hand to Travis. The touch of her cool flesh did strange things to him. She smiled at Clinton. "How are you today, Clinton Vaughn?"

"Just fine, Theresa. You are more lovely than ever."

She flushed a little as he tilted his head to one side and studied her. She walked back to her grandfather and stood beside his great chair, one slim hand on his shoulder.

James Morris placed a gnarled hand atop hers, hiding it from view. "Captain Walker seems to think we of Santa Theresa cannot defend ourselves, Granddaughter."

She smiled a little. "These are hard times, Grandfather. There has never been anything like this before. If the captain offers his help I am sure he knows we need it. We should be grateful."

The *alcalde* opened his mouth, but she interrupted him swiftly. "Remember, Grandfather, that the country is at war. There are few troops available to help us. Cuchillo Rojo rides the hills with many warriors. The people here are frightened. They cannot leave now. We stay here and fight for our homes. Only fools would turn away offers of help."

Clinton turned his head to hide a grin. He winked at Travis. James Morris cleared his throat. "Well, perhaps I was too hasty,

Captain Walker. I am a man who has always taken care of myself and my people. Please do what you can to help us. Tell me what measures you require for the defense of the town, and I will see that they are carried through."

"Thank you, Major Morris."

"It is we who should thank you, Captain Walker," said Theresa quietly.

Travis looked at her in a different light now. There was strength in the young woman, a far greater strength than he had realized. The candlelight seemed to bring out the soft tones of her flesh and accentuate the darkness of her hair. It served, too, to give Travis the vague impression that he was looking at a full-length oil painting by one of the masters.

Travis picked up his hat. "If you'll excuse me, sir, and you, Miss Morris, I'd like to inspect the town with Mr. Vaughn."

The mayor nodded. "A man of quick action. That is good. There are too many young men these days who are not men of action, as I once was."

"You still are, Grandfather," said Theresa Morris. She pulled the serape higher on his legs. "I'll escort these gentlemen to the door."

Travis opened the door, and Clint Vaughn stood aside to let her pass. She was taller

93

than Travis had realized. A faint, almost indistinguishable odor of perfume came to him. Travis glanced at the old man as he closed the door. James Morris sat in his great chair, bolt upright, his strong hands clasping his ebony and silver cane. He was looking straight at Travis. Travis nodded, but the old man did not move. It was almost as though he were a figure without life. It gave Travis an eerie feeling.

Theresa Morris smiled up at Travis. "He is old," she said, "and sometimes set in his ways. But he loves the people of Santa Theresa and the town itself. It is not easy for him to realize that his life's work may be wiped out in one Apache attack."

"It won't be!" said Clint heartily.

Travis glanced at the quartermaster. Clint was whistling in the dark. Theresa stopped at the front door. She placed a hand on Clint's arm. "You don't have to worry about me, Clint. I know what might happen."

"You should have left here long ago," said Travis angrily.

She shook her dark head. "My grandfather would not leave, nor will I as long as he remains. We have only the two of us. Each gives strength to the other in many ways."

Clint opened the great door. The outer light

94

struck against Theresa's face, and again Travis realized how beautiful she was. In candlelight or sunlight her beauty was the same. Travis and Clint walked out beneath the ramada. "If there is anything you want done, Captain Walker," she said, "you have only to tell me and I'll see that it is done."

Clint grinned. "You are now the *alcalde*, Theresa?"

"No. But there are many things I can do to help him. Good morning, gentlemen."

They both bowed. The door clicked shut behind them. Travis was silent as he walked out into the brilliant sunlight. They walked toward the sagging *torreon*. Clint lit a cigar. "Say," he said, offhand, "you never did tell me if you were married."

"I'm not."

Clint nodded. "I can usually tell."

"What's bothering you, Clint?"

The quartermaster looked back at the house. "Nothing. I'm just the second son of a second son, Travis."

"So?"

"I can foresee things."

"You better foresee the Apache attack."

Travis stopped in front of the *torreon*. He looked back at the rambling house they had just left. He had a feeling he had left part of himself back there, something he would never fully possess again as long as he lived.

Travis bent his head to walk into the *torreon*. He stood in the center of the littered floor and looked at the sunlight streaming through the great cracks. A rack of rusty *escopetas* stood to one side. Spiders had made their homes about the old weapons. A rickety ladder rose to enter a trap door in the second floor. Travis tested it with his feet. The bottom rung snapped off. "Jesus," said Travis. "Can't the old man see the condition this town is in for defense?"

"No."

"Is he that bullheaded or just plain stupid?"

"No. Didn't you notice anything about him?"

"He's a cripple."

"In more ways than one. He's also stone-blind, Travis."

Travis turned to look at the quartermaster. "What?"

"I meant to tell you."

Travis shook his head. "A fort commanded by a bumbling old fool, a town falling apart, a crippled and blind *alcalde*. What next, I wonder?"

"Cuchillo Rojo," said Clint quietly.

They looked at each other. "Well," Travis said dryly, "I always wanted to be a soldier."

Clint nodded. "Me, too."

"Then we'd better play the part, *amigo*."

"Yes. What do we do now?"

"Get some of these lazy *paisanos* to get to work on this ramshackle *torreon*. Find out how they're fixed for weapons and ammunition. Get a squad or two to help garrison the place."

"The *torreon* can be patched up and if they need weapons we can draw them from my stores. As far as letting Major Lester allow troops to be garrisoned here – well, I think you'll have a hell of a time convincing him of that."

"If I had my way I'd move these people to the fort or else move the garrison here."

Clint shrugged. "Sure. Sure. But you don't have your way at all. It's going to take a lot of convincing talk to allow me to issue weapons to these people."

They walked out into the sunlight. A drunk lay atop a pile of straw in the hot shade of the *torreon*. From a nearby *cantina* came the soft strumming of a guitar. Two men sat in the shade of a crude thatched shelter industriously playing monte. A peon walked across the plaza carrying a fighting cock under his left arm. The town looked as though there was only peace in New Mexico.

A scarf of signal smoke drifted up from a hill far behind the town, staining the clear blue sky. A deadly warning of danger for anyone to see, but Santa Theresa slept in the hot sun and dreamed of nothing but peace.

Travis placed a hand on Clint's shoulder. "Go about your business," he said. "I'll look around. How long will it take you?"

"No more than half an hour."

"Get moving then."

Clint Vaughn strode off toward the south end of town. Travis walked about, eying the houses. Some of them could be put into shape for defense. He looked at the rambling adobe of James Morris. There were several outbuildings in good repair behind it. Perhaps the townspeople could use the house as a citadel while others defended the *torreon*. There was a good field of cross fire possible between them if one old sagging adobe was leveled. The great house likely had a large cistern in it.

Travis walked along the row of *cantinas*. Bold women eyed him as he passed. Some of them flirted their well-padded hips at him. He could hear men laughing and talking in the *cantinas*.

Clint came to meet Travis. "Do you have a notebook?" asked Travis.

"Yes."

"*Bueno!* Now write these instructions down for the mayor – I want the *torreon* reënforced and repaired as much as possible; the ladders are to be replaced; every cistern in town must be filled to the brim; I want that old adobe between the *torreon* and the mayor's house leveled so that there is no defilade between both buildings; every man in town is to clean and furbish his weapons.

"I'll try to get some troops here. Their commanding officer will be responsible for seeing that the weapons are ready in case they are needed. He will also inspect the cisterns to see that they are full and will make sure that adobe is torn down."

Clint wrote rapidly and then looked up. "Anything else?"

"No. Wait – you might add that if these conditions are not met within the next few days I will ask Major Lester to declare martial law."

"These people won't like that."

"To hell with that! We're trying to save their lives!"

Clint nodded. "What do I do with this memorandum?"

"Send it to the mayor."

Clint got a small boy to deliver the message. The two officers mounted their horses and rode from the town, followed by the cynical eyes of the gamblers beneath the brush shelter. One of them laughed aloud. It was the little man Vince.

CHAPTER SIX

There was no sound of musketry as Travis and Clint approached Fort Joslyn. As they entered the fort quadrangle they saw a line of troopers, under the charge of Sergeant Ellis, practicing with their heavy Chicopee sabers. Thrusts and parries, right and left moulinets, were being done by the sweating cavalrymen. "Sergeant Ellis!" called out Travis.

The big noncom approached Travis, then saluted him with his saber. "Yes, sir?"

"Surely you haven't finished target practice?"

"We didn't even start, sir. Captain Cass instructed us to practice with the saber."

"A hell of a lot of good that will do us," muttered Clint Vaughn.

Travis looked up at the brilliant sun. It would have been hot enough on the target range, but this was sheer idiocy – men swinging those heavy blades in blasting summer heat. "Give them a ten-minute rest," said Travis. "I'll have further orders for you in a few minutes."

"Yes, sir!"

Travis swung down from his horse. An

orderly led it off. Clint rode to his quartermaster warehouse and looked back at Travis. He shrugged as he dismounted.

Travis entered headquarters. Major Lester was seated at his desk, poring over a sheaf of papers. He looked up and returned Travis' salute. "Well?" he asked.

Travis leaned forward. "My instructions for the garrison were for them to have target practice this morning, sir."

Lester nodded. "I know. I countermanded them on the suggestion of Captain Cass."

"May I ask why, sir?"

"We cannot afford to waste ammunition, Captain."

"We'll be wasting a great deal of ammunition in an Apache attack if the men do not get practice."

Lester smiled thinly. "Our troopers can ride them down with the *arme blanche* and the pistol. The saber and hand gun are all a good trooper needs to attack with."

"Perhaps. But what of the infantry, sir?"

"They have other duties at present."

Futile anger swept over Travis. The man before him lived in a little world of his own with boundaries he had set up for himself, playing at being a field soldier, afraid of the responsibility of command, yet determined

101

that he be recognized as the final authority on all matters.

Enos Lester did not seem to notice Travis' anger. "What did you learn in Santa Theresa?" he asked.

"The town is practically unprotected. The people seem to be torn between their fear of the Apaches and their love of comfort. The *cantinas* are doing a rushing business. It seems to me that the people have turned to amusement to throw a temporary shield between them and inevitable disaster."

Enos Lester smiled. "Come, come, Captain Walker, it can't be as bad as that. A soldier must be an optimist, not a dismal pessimist."

"I have promised to send some troops into the town. I have left orders for the cisterns to be filled. The old *torreon* is to be repaired. Weapons are to be cleaned and readied for a possible attack."

"The town is not under martial law, sir! We have no right to interfere in civil government."

"There doesn't seem to be much civil government there. James Morris is a cripple, and blind to boot. He knows little of the condition of the town defenses."

"He is a capable man, well beloved by all." Lester steepled his pudgy fingers on his chest. "You said you promised troops? By whose authority, sir?"

"I assumed you would send them, sir."

Lester sat bolt upright. "You *assumed?* By what *right* do you assume? *I* am in command here, sir!"

God help us all, thought Travis.

There was an angry flush on Lester's face. Any time his authority was questioned he seemed to lose his reason.

"Sir," said Travis patiently, "if Santa Theresa is attacked the blame will be placed upon you. It is part of the major's district of command. Mayor Morris is well known and respected throughout New Mexico. If anything happens to him and his town, the finger of guilt will point at one man – Major Enos Lester."

Lester sagged a little in his chair. Travis' opening shot had struck home.

Travis continued. "There are two alternatives, other than sending a detail to Santa Theresa, sir – the first is to evacuate the townspeople and bring them here under your protection; the second is to move the garrison to Santa Theresa, abandoning Fort Joslyn!"

Lester waved a hand. "Both of them are impossible. I have no authority to command the evacuation of Santa Theresa. Then again, we have no room for those people here. Our water supply is not sufficient. I cannot abandon this post."

"Then we must send troops to help the people of Santa Theresa."

Lester fiddled with his pen. He yawned and looked out of the window. He scratched his throat. "How many men?"

"At least two squads under the command of an officer."

Lester cracked his knuckles.

"Well, Major?"

The major looked up. "Very well. Send Captain Cass in command of the detail."

"Rather a high rank to command two squads."

"It requires more ability than just the command of two squads. It requires enough rank to make those people listen and obey. I'm sure that Captain Cass will have the qualities to deal with them."

"Very well, sir."

"Is there anything else?"

"I would like to send some couriers to the closest fort on the Rio Grande."

"That would be Fort Craig. That is about one hundred and fifty miles from here."

"We can pick the men, sir. I'd suggest sending three of them by different routes."

"Even if they *do* get through, they will accomplish nothing. No troops will be dispatched to us."

"That was not my thought, sir. I think the

major should request authority to abandon this post and to evacuate Santa Theresa. If we get that authority we can travel in column to the Rio Grande."

"Too dangerous, sir!"

"Is it possibly any more dangerous than staying *here?*"

Enos Lester wet his purplish lips. Then he eyed Travis. "Very well, Captain. Pick your men and send them out. God help them."

"There is nothing else we can do, Major."

"Get to it then."

Travis left headquarters. Major Lester walked to the window. "They'll never make it, Captain Walker," he said quietly. He laughed, a crafty look in his pale eyes.

The three troopers stood by their horses, listening to Travis' final instructions. It was dusk, and lamplight gleamed in the windows of the buildings. "I asked you men to volunteer," said Travis, "because I wanted the men who went to know what they were up against. It is a dangerous mission."

"No more dangerous than it is here, sir," said Amos Corby, a lanky Vermonter.

"Perhaps," said Travis.

"I'm sick of sitting around here waiting for Cuchillo to swoop down on us," said John Nolan, a quiet Pennsylvanian.

"I'm with you, John," said the third courier, Benson Duryea, a squat trooper from Kentucky.

"You three will ride together until you reach the vicinity of Red Mountain," said Travis. "Then you separate. Corby will tend north toward Cooks Peak, then skirt the mountains and continue north to about the vicinity of Fort Craig, thence east to Fort Craig.

"Nolan will ride toward Goodsight Peak, skirt it to the east, thence past Sunday Cone, thence up the west bank of the Rio Grande to Fort Craig.

"Duryea, you will head east to Massacre Peak, thence toward Sierra de las Uvas, skirting them to the north, thence crossing the Rio Grande to follow Jorado del Muerte north to the vicinity of the Lava Flow. You'll have to ford the Rio Grande at Valverde, north of the fort and return south down the west bank of the Rio."

"The long way around for Benson," said Corby, with a wide grin.

"Hole up during the day," said Travis. "Travel from dusk until just before dawn. Don't wear out your mounts. You'll have to travel slowly to conserve them. You've been told of the water holes, and have sketch maps. You have your extra canteens and pistols?"

The men nodded.

"Good!" Travis shook each of them by the hand. "Remember – the lives of many people and your fellow soldiers may depend upon you. I'll promise two stripes to each of you if you're successful."

"Or a wooden cross and a pat in the face with a shovel," said Nolan quietly.

"On your way," said Travis.

He walked to the gate with them and watched as they led their mounts quietly into the wash that traversed the desert in a northeasterly direction. They had muffled their horses' hoofs with soft leather boots. In a few minutes there was no sight nor sound of them.

"We'll never see those three again," a sentry said.

"Shut up," said a corporal.

Far out across the desert to the west, a coyote gave voice. The howl died away, echoing faintly in the hills.

Charles Cass had formed his detail near the gate. They were to travel in two wagons, and Travis had ordered that they travel at night to avoid detection by the Apaches. It wasn't likely that the keen-eared Mimbrenos would miss hearing the passage of the wagons, but it was a chance that had to be taken.

Cass looked at Travis. "I'll leave now," he said.

Travis nodded. "Report to James Morris. You'll have to be quartered in the town. Perhaps the mayor will take you in."

Cass wet his lips. "I'll see to that."

"You have your instructions. If you want to say good-by to your wife, go ahead and do it."

Cass laughed. "Her? She doesn't give a damn *where* I go."

"Move out then."

The wagons had been prepared for the trip. Axles dripped with grease, and rags had been wound between the wheels and the axles to deaden sound. Harness chains, too, had been wrapped to prevent their jingling. Leather boots had been wrapped about the horse's hoofs.

The two wagons rolled softly out onto the road and vanished from sight. Travis stood there for a time, listening to the soughing of the night wind through the brush, half expecting to hear a burst of gunfire, but it did not come. So far, so good.

Travis made his rounds. He had ordered that all outward facing windows be shuttered. No lights were to be shown an hour after dusk. Here and there, lights blinked out as he walked about the quiet post. He checked the sentries, then walked to the high-walled corral. Two sentries stood at the corral gate. They had orders that one of them must patrol the outer walls of the corral every hour. The civilians were quiet enough. Travis' treatment of Ben Joad and his two drunken companions had had a sobering effect on them.

It was after nine o'clock when Travis finished his thorough inspection. He walked to his quarters, glancing at the quartermaster warehouse. Clint was hard at work on his accounts, and would be for some hours. Travis opened the door, then closed it behind him. He slid the bar across. He had experienced Apache sneak raids before. At one post two officers had been found dead in their beds with slashed throats because they had been foolish enough to leave their outer doors open to the night breeze.

Travis unbuckled his gun belt and hung it over a chair. He stripped off shirt and undershirt and threw them in a corner. He wiped his upper body with a towel, then reached for a bottle. Something scraped in the rear of the big room. He snatched his Colt free from its holster and cocked it as a figure took shape in the darkness. His finger drew up the trigger slack, and then he noticed the strong odor of jasmine.

"I've been waiting for you, Travis," said Evelyn Cass. She came closer. The muzzle of the big Colt touched her soft belly. Cold sweat broke out on Travis. He lowered the Colt and let down the hammer. "For God's sake!" he said huskily. "That was a foolish thing to do!"

"I'm sorry I startled you, Travis," she said softly.

"What do you want?"

She smiled in the dimness. "I wanted to ask you about Santa Theresa. It's been some time since I've been there."

Travis shrugged. "It's just the same, I imagine."

"At least there is some life there."

"You're safer here."

"Why, Charles will defend the town, won't he?" There was veiled sarcasm in her voice.

Travis threw his Colt onto his cot and reached for a fresh shirt. He drew it over his head and buttoned it. "You'd better get out of here," he said quietly.

She tilted her head to one side. "Why? Do I make you nervous?"

"No. But you know post rules. If anyone should find you in here, there would be some nasty talk resulting from it."

"I'm worried. Clint won't be here for hours. Major Lester is already in bed. The other officers are playing poker in the mess."

"You made sure of everything before you came here, then?"

She laughed. "I hadn't thought of a rendezvous, Travis."

He stuffed his shirt tails into his trousers. "Leave by the back door," he said.

"I'd like a drink."

"No."

She reached for the bottle and tilted it to her full lips. She drank deeply, then placed the bottle on the table. "Do I shock you, Captain Walker?"

"Get out of here."

"Your virtue is safe enough."

"Damn you!"

She swayed a little, and then Travis realized she had been doing considerable drinking. She gripped his left arm and tried to pull him close to her. Then, suddenly, she threw her arms about his neck and drew him close, searching for his lips with hers. She found them and crushed him to her. Her full body pressed hard against his, and he knew damned well she had nothing on beneath her thin summer gown. Her mouth tasted of liquor as she forced it against his, bruising his lips.

Travis pulled her arms from around his neck and pushed her back. "Go!" he said.

She staggered a little as she reached for the bottle. He took it away from her, then walked to the back door. He threw it open. For a moment she stared at him, and then she smoothed down her dark hair. "All right," she said thickly. She brushed heavily against

111

him as she walked outside. Then she turned and looked at him. "Sir Galahad," she said sarcastically. She laughed softly as she walked unsteadily toward her own quarters.

Travis closed and barred the door. He whistled softly. She was a bundle of woman, all right. He picked up the bottle and drank deeply. It seemed to him as though he could taste her mouth from the rim of the bottle.

A woman came from the sanitary sinks at the far end of the quarters row. She watched Evelyn Cass stagger a little as she walked up on the rear porch of her quarters. The woman smiled thinly, then hurried toward the civilian quarters. It was the woman who had been mixed up in the drunken brawl when Travis had disarmed and beaten Ben Joad.

Evelyn Cass walked into her stifling bedroom and picked up a cutglass decanter. She drank from it, then hurled it into the beehive fireplace. The decanter smashed, filling the room with the pungent odor of strong brandy. She stripped herself and threw herself on the damp bed. She passed her hands over her full body. "Damn him," she said drunkenly.

Travis pulled off his shirt and boots and sat by the window for a breath of fresh night air. Now and then he sipped at the bottle. It had been quite some time since he had been with a woman, and she hadn't been in a class with Evelyn. He almost wished he had sent some other officer to Santa Theresa, but in a way he was glad to get rid of Charlie Cass. He wondered if Evelyn would find another officer on the post willing to tumble with her.

Travis was still sitting there when Clint Vaughn came to the quarters. Clint pulled off his damp shirt and undershirt and reached for the bottle. "I feel like I've been in a Turkish bath," he said.

Travis nodded.

"What's bothering you?"

"Nothing."

Clint eyed Travis. Then he raised his head. "Damned if I don't think I smell jasmine," he said.

"You're loco."

"The hell I am!"

"Take a drink and forget it."

Clint took another drink. He stood up and walked to the washstand at the rear of the room. He lit a candle and poured water into a basin. Then he saw something lying on the stand, and he picked it up. It was a filmy handkerchief. He raised it to his nostrils, and inhaled. Then he looked over his shoulder at Travis. "I'll be damned!" he said.

"What's wrong now?" asked Travis.

Clint stuffed the handkerchief into a drawer. "Bugs in the water," he said quickly.

Travis grinned. "Just taking a cooling swim, Clint."

"Yeah. Yeah."

Clint washed himself and opened the rear door to pitch out the water. "The musketoons have been weighted as ordered," he said.

"At least that's one thing I accomplished."

Clint closed the door and glanced at the drawer into which he had stuffed the perfumed handkerchief. "Yeah," he said softly.

Later, as they lay on their cots, Clint raised himself on an elbow and looked at Travis. "I've heard Charlie Cass was more than willing to go to Santa Theresa."

"He seemed happy enough about it."

Clint lay back on his cot. "Charlie will have a time for himself. He likes his liquor and his women. I told you that before. I remember you wondered about that, with the woman he has already."

"So?"

"Nothing."

Travis looked through the darkness toward Clint. Then he rested his head on his hot pillow and closed his eyes. He listened to the night sounds – the soft whispering of the wind about the quarters; the bawling of a mule from the corral; the fluttering of the flag halyards against the warped pole; the tread of a sentry making his rounds. He tried to think of lovely Theresa Morris, but the oval face of Evelyn Cass seemed always to get in between Travis and the face of Theresa.

CHAPTER SEVEN

The roar of a rifle snapped Travis Walker into wakefulness. He sat up, pulled on trousers and shirt, then yanked on his boots. Clint was alert, dressing swiftly. "Came from near the corral!" he said.

They buckled on their gun belts and rushed out onto the dim parade ground. It was almost dawn. A trooper darted between two buildings, raised his musketoon and fired into the darkness. The thud of hoofs came back on the wind, and a derisive yell floated back with the sounds of the hoofs.

Travis cocked his Colt and headed for the corral.

"Corporal of the Guard! Post Number Six!" roared a sentry.

Travis saw something lying on the ground at one side of the corral. It was a trooper.

115

His chest had a curiously flattened look. The corral gate was sagging on one hinge, and the bitter smell of dust was mingled with the acrid odor of burnt gunpowder. The guard came upon the double. "What is it, Cassidy?" yelled the corporal.

Cassidy grounded his musketoon. "Me and Fletcher was in front of the corral gate. Fletch hears a noise. He goes to open the gate when all of a sudden the damned gate crashes open. A horse comes racing out with an Apache on his back. Poor Fletch gets run down. I snapped a shot at the red devil, but he was in the clear, he was."

"What shall we do, sir?" asked the corporal.

"Stay where you are!"

Travis walked into the corral. The horses and mules milled about, whinnying and braying. Dust was thick in the air. Travis looked at the gate. The thick leather hinges had been slit by a knife until they were hanging by a mere half inch of leather. That last half inch had been ripped through.

Travis edged past the excited animals until he reached the rear wall. A rawhide rope hung down from the top of the wall. Clint Vaughn came up behind Travis. "What happened, do you think?"

Travis eased down his pistol hammer and

holstered the Colt. "Simple enough. A buck came over the wall, slashed the gate hinges until they were hanging by a thread, then picked out the best mount he could find and crashed it through the gate."

"But why one horse?"

Travis turned. "To show us what they can do if they want to. Psychology, Clint. Damned diabolical psychology."

" 'Twas Cuchillo Rojo on the horse," said Cassidy.

"You're sure?" asked Clint.

"Certainly, sir! I know his face, the dirty, murderin' bastard!"

Travis walked to the gate of the corral. "You made your rounds, Cassidy?"

"Yes, sir."

Clint shook his head. "I don't see how he did it," he said.

"He waited until the sentry went past, then threw over his rope. Perfect timing."

"Shall we turn out the post?"

"They'll all be awake now. There's nothing more we can do."

Clint loked down at the dead trooper. "Poor bastard," he said. "He probably never knew what happened."

"It's just the beginning," said Travis quietly. "From now on he'll whittle at us until he's ready to strike for keeps."

Tension seemed to settle about Fort Joslyn that day. The sentries stared at the surrounding hills until their eyes ached. Each wind devil that arose on the flats was eyed narrowly, as though the dust were rising from the hoofs of Apache mounts. But there was no sign of the Mimbrenos. No smoke stained the clear sky. Cuchillo Rojo had done his work well. He had the garrison on edge now, and he would keep it that way.

At noon mess Norval DeSantis seemed restless. He toyed with his food. "What's bothering you, De?" asked Ken Carlie.

"Those damned Apaches! I'd like to take a patrol up into the hills and run Cuchillo to earth."

Carlie laughed. "You wouldn't see one of them until they opened fire and cut you to pieces."

"I'm not afraid to go."

"No one said you were."

DeSantis looked down the table. "I'd like to ask the major's permission to patrol the hills west of here," he said.

"Absolutely not!" snapped Lester as he helped himself to more stew.

DeSantis emptied his coffee cup. "Are we to sit here like roosting chickens and get knocked off our perches without a fight?"

"You may get all the fight you want without leaving here," said Travis dryly.

There was a sneer on DeSantis' face. "United States Army soldiers sitting here behind walls, letting a pack of half naked savages put the fear of God into us. Two troopers shot down without a fight, and we still sit here!"

"That is enough, Mr. DeSantis," Lester said, with his mouth full. His jaws worked steadily on his food.

"It sickens me," said DeSantis.

Travis looked up. "Run your gun crew through drill this afternoon. That'll take some of the disgust out of you," he said coldly.

De Santis opened his mouth, then closed it as he looked into Travis' hard eyes. He looked at Enos Lester, who was forking more food into his mouth. Then he stood up. "I'd like to be excused, Major," he said.

Lester waved his fork. "Granted," he said thickly.

DeSantis left the mess. Martin Newkirk filled his cup. "The young eagle wants to try his wings."

"He'll get them clipped quickly enough," said Clint Vaughn.

"The boy is hot-blooded," said the major as he ladled jam onto a piece of bread. "I was

119

that way myself once. One good bloodletting and he'll cool off."

Travis looked at the major. He wondered if Enos Lester had ever seen a good bloodletting. Travis was willing to bet the old man would crack completely and let Travis take command if an attack occurred, but until he cracked he'd probably raise hell with the morale of the already shaky garrison.

A trooper came to the door. "Captain Travis," he said. "Baconora is back."

"I'll see him in my quarters."

Lester jerked his head. "He'll report here," he said. "We'd *all* like to hear what he has to say."

Travis nodded to the trooper. "Tell him to come in here."

Baconora padded into the room, bringing with him a strong aura of stale sweat and rank tobacco. He touched his hatbrim with his right hand.

Major Lester turned in his seat. "Well?" he asked.

Baconora squatted on his heels and wiped his ragged mustache both ways. "Cuchillo had a big palaver in the hills night before last. Mimbrenos mostly, with some Chiricahuas, but all top warriors."

"Chiricahuas?" asked Lester. "It isn't

120

likely they'd be over here. You were probably mistaken, sir."

Baconora's reddish eyes surveyed the major. "I said they *was* Chiricahuas there."

"Bosh! How could you tell? They all look alike."

Baconora spat into a spittoon. The metal rang softly with the impact of the tobacco juice. "Not to anyone what knows them, they don't."

Lester sniffed. He filled his coffee cup and slopped a little of the coffee down his chin as he drank.

"Go on, Baconora," urged Travis.

"Well, it seems as though Cuchillo is talking big about having Fort Joslyn and Santa Theresa under his greasy thumb. Looks like he's rallying as many warriors as he can."

"They'll sit out there in the hills," said Lester. "They won't dare attack."

"No," said the scout quietly. "When they meet and palaver and then begin to gather, they got plans on their minds. They ain't like white men, who'll keep up a force for weeks and months and then strike. When they start gathering you know damned well they mean to attack, for they can't keep together for long periods of time like we can."

"How many warriors do you think he can muster?" asked Travis.

"I saw about fifty or sixty in the hills."

Major Lester laughed. "We can handle them."

Baconora shifted his chew. "I said I *saw* fifty or sixty. Cuchillo has warriors watching this fort and others watching Santa Theresa. He has war parties raiding as far east as the Rio Grande and other parties raiding down into Chihuahua. When the time comes, he'll have enough warriors for his purpose."

Major Lester paled a little. His eyes seemed to dart about the table. "Well, gentlemen, we must keep a stiff upper lip and gird our loins. I want no fear amongst you."

The officers looked at him. There was some fear in each of them in varying quantities, for none of them were fools, but each of them knew that Enos Lester was more afraid by far than any of them.

The major stood up. "To work, gentlemen." He left the mess. Travis walked outside, followed by Baconora. They walked over to Travis' quarters. Travis handed the scout a bottle of mezcal. "I don't know how you got close enough to Cuchillo's camp to learn what you did," he said, "but it's worth a bottle of mezcal to me."

Baconora grinned crookedly. "I just use Apache methods," he said.

Travis nodded. "Take it easy for a day, and

122

then report to me. Don't leave the post."

Baconora patted the bottle. "Not with this to keep me company, I won't."

"I have three couriers out trying for the Rio Grande."

The scout's head jerked. "When did they leave?"

"Last evening."

"They'll never make it."

"We had to take the risk."

"Ain't no risk in it; the throw of the dice was against them before they left. You won't see those men again. Not alive, anyways."

"You seem pretty sure."

"I am."

"We'll wait three days. At the end of that time, I want you to trail them to see if they got out of this country."

"Yeh. I'll do it. Won't do any good, though. You'll see. Maybe even before I go." Baconora walked to the door, saluted Travis carelessly, then left the quarters, leaving a feeling of deep apprehension hovering within Travis.

Travis went to the window and watched DeSantis drilling his men on the use of the howitzer. The sun glinted from the highly polished brass piece. It wouldn't be of much value as a killing instrument, but cannon had always had a terrifying effect on

Indians. They hated the wagon-guns worse than anything. The howitzer might be of value in a defense, but on the offensive it would be impractical, because the Apaches certainly would never allow it to get within effective shooting range. The howitzer was one of Enos Lester's pet projects at Fort Joslyn. The bumbling major, with all his years of quartermastering and paper work, seemed to think he was commanding a force of the three arms of the service – infantry, cavalry and artillery. It wasn't a force in any sense; it was hardly a representation of the three arms.

Travis shook his head. Perhaps the major had dreams of leading cavalry, infantry and artillery in some miniature battle, preparatory to taking command of his ambition, the combat brigade.

A lean man walked past the drilling gunners. It was Ben Joad, his face swathed in bandages. No charges had been pressed against him, because Major Lester didn't want the civilians to take up Ben Joad's fight with the military. There was enough friction already at Fort Joslyn. Travis had known men of Joad's stamp before. The man would never forget or forgive Travis for what he had done.

Travis walked outside and walked past the corral. He stopped fifty yards from the corral and looked about. He had ideas of having a redoubt built to protect the fort, because the fort was such in name only, hardly able to be defended by the small garrison.

There was a low knoll a hundred yards from the fort. It overlooked the Santa Theresa road and was some fifteen feet higher than the site of the fort. Rifle fire from the knoll could effectively cover the corral, preventing the Apaches from attacking it. A redoubt would also be able to afford a sweeping fire along the west and south sides of the fort.

Travis went back to the post and got an axe and several short lengths of boards. He returned to the knoll and paced off an area about fifty feet square. He hammered in stakes for boundary markers, planning an octagonal redoubt. Perhaps he could persuade the major to have the howitzer mounted in the planned redoubt on a plank platform. Grape or canister fired from the small artillery piece could sweep the western and southern approaches to the fort. Such redoubts had already been started at Fort Yuma before he had left there.

Clint Vaughn approached Travis. "What are you doing?" he asked. "Staking out a claim?"

Travis grinned. "Certainly. This is a solid mound of silver."

Clint lit a cigar and eyed the stakes. "A redoubt?"

"You guessed it."

"You think the major will allow you to have it built?"

"He'd better."

"I wouldn't bet on it."

"Why?"

"He doesn't believe in pick and shovel work. He thinks the United States Army is far too valorous to hide behind heaps of dirt."

Travis wiped the sweat from his face. "If Cuchillo Rojo is the tactician I think he is, he'd see the military value of the knoll at once. He could place a dozen good marksmen on here and pepper hell out of us at will."

"You forget the major has his inestimable howitzer. With it he thinks he is invincible."

"He'd have to roll it out into the open to get a clear field of fire. By the time the gun was in battery the gunners would all be shot down by fire from this knoll."

"You won't convince him of that, Travis."

Travis hurled the axe at one of his stakes. The axe struck true and hard, splitting the stake. "The man is an utter fool!"

Clint waved a hand in warning and jerked his head toward the fort. Major Lester was walking toward them through the brush.

"Gentlemen! Gentlemen!" he called. "What are you doing out here?"

"This is your chance, Travis," said Clint *sotto voce.*

The major puffed up the slope and returned their salutes. "What is this? Are you planning a garden here?"

Travis shook his head. "We need a redoubt here, sir. We can put the howitzer into position here and cover the western and southern sides of the post, as well as the corral, with howitzer and rifle fire."

The major shook his head. "It will not be necessary to exhaust the men by digging under this hot sun. I have already made plans for an effective defense of the fort."

"Yes, sir?" asked Travis.

Lester nodded complacently. "We will place the howitzer on the roof of the quarter-master warehouse."

Clint Vaughn looked away. He relit his cigar. His shoulders seemed to be shaking a little.

Travis looked at the warehouse. "It might not be possible to depress the howitzer enough to sweep the area close in to the fort, sir."

"I do not intend to let the enemy approach *that* close, captain. When the time comes, we will meet them with saber and pistol. Our infantry can defend the buildings and, if necessary, attack the enemy on foot."

"But if they do manage to get close to the buildings, sir," said Travis patiently, "the howitzer will be of no value whatsoever."

Major Lester shook his head. "You know cavalry tactics, I am sure, sir, but you must leave the proper handling of other arms to me. We can raise the trail of the howitzer with blocks and fire close to the buildings. Simple, is it not?"

"Very simple," said Travis dryly.

The major nodded in satisfaction. "You see my wisdom then."

"Quite, sir. But I still believe this knoll, if in our hands, would be the key to the defense of the fort. On the other hand, if the Apaches gain possession of it they will have a fine field of fire into the fort."

"But the howitzer will drive them from the knoll, will it not?"

"The gunners will be almost completely exposed up on that roof, sir. Besides, the shock of recoil might weaken the roof to such an extent that it will collapse."

Enos Lester waved a hand. "The roof will hold, sir. I do not like to hear talk of defense. As a junior officer with a career ahead of him in the cavalry, you should think of *offense*, rather than *defense*."

It was no use, thought Travis. The man was

hidebound, and would brook no arguments against his plans. His very lack of fighting experience had probably convinced him he could do no wrong. A veteran soldier would have examined and evaluated all possibilities of an enemy coup, but not Enos Lester.

Major Lester placed a hand on Travis' shoulder. "Remember, Captain, that I too have studied Vauban. I know all about parapets, epaulements, redans, redoubts, glacis and chevaux-de-frise. But you are not an engineer, and neither am I. We are field soldiers, and, I might add, *fighting* soldiers, not men who put their trust in heaps of earth and in the defensive. Remember that well. Now – there is work to be done. Mr. Vaughn, your post of duty is in the quarter-master warehouse. Captain Walker, I'm sure you have many details to superintend. To work, gentlemen, to work!"

Major Lester bustled off down the hill with the brim of his Kossuth hat flopping at every stride. At the base of the hill, he clenched the hilt of his sword with his left hand and balled his right hand. He shook it vigorously toward the hazy hills. "Cuchillo!" he cried. "Just match swords' points with Major Enos Lester. Just try!" Then he hurried past the corral and vanished from sight.

Clint Vaughn took his cigar from his

mouth. "Well, I'll be damned," he said.

Travis picked up the axe and hefted it. "It seems as though we are, Clint. *It seems as though we are.*"

They walked down the low hillock together.

Major Lester, a far cry from the man who spent much time doctoring himself and soaking his feet in mustard baths, spent the long hot afternoon supervising the placing of the howitzer atop the quartermaster warehouse. Sergeant Ellis, a jack of all trades, rigged shear poles to hoist the barrel and carriage of the stubby little weapon to its position on the flat roof of the large building.

Norval DeSantis said hardly a word all afternoon, other than those which were necessary for commands. Major Lester was quite pleased with himself, and spent much time in asides to any officer and enlisted man who got within earshot, explaining the brilliance of his stratagem in placing the cannon in such a position. He saw to it that shot, grape and canister, with the necessary powder and friction tubes, were hauled up to the roof and placed in a wooden structure Corporal Covello had fabricated. A trooper, temporarily assigned to the artillery detail, was to stand guard beside the howitzer.

Major Lester ordered the preparation of heavy wooden blocks, which could be placed beneath the trail of the gun in such a way as to elevate the trail and thus depress the barrel for close-in shooting.

Clint Vaughn walked about inside his stuffy warehouse among the piles of boxes, sacks and barrels, eying the roof over his head. Now and then bits of adobe pattered down upon the stores.

Travis kept himself busy with the myriad of details an executive officer is responsible for, but, now and then, he couldn't help viewing the progress of Major Lester's brain child. Travis only hoped that Charles Cass was as energetic as the major in seeing to the defense of Santa Theresa, according to the instructions laid down by Travis. God help Santa Theresa if the major went there and used his wild reasoning in the preparation of the town's defenses.

A mild sort of madness seemed to have come over Enos Lester, as though, by his intense supervision of activities, he could forestall the mysterious movements of Cuchillo Rojo. But there was no sign of the Apaches. No smoke against the clear skies, no dust rising from the desert floor, no sight of lone Apache scouts on the distant hill slopes. It was as though the Mimbrenos

131

and their Chiricahua allies had completely vanished from the area.

When night came it was as silent as the grave; an apt simile, thought Travis Walker grimly as he made his evening rounds. The sentries were alert. There was too much tension at Fort Joslyn for them to be otherwise.

The moon had not yet risen when Travis left his quarters. Ken Carlie was officer of the guard. Travis knew the man was capable and conscientious, but the responsibility for the safety of the fort really rested on Travis. He walked toward the corral and heard the sharp challenge of the sentry. He looked up toward the roof of the warehouse and saw the trooper on guard pacing back and forth near his charge, the little brass howitzer. Travis walked toward the gate. The moon was beginning to tint the eastern heights.

The gate sentry was standing behind a buttress of the guardhouse, staring out into the darkness beyond the gate. He turned to see Travis. "I thought I heard something out there," he said.

Travis stared into the darkness. He could vaguely make out the indistinct outlines of clumps of brush. It was a job he planned to order soon – the cutting of all brush within at least a hundred yards of the post.

The sentry leaned forward. "There *is* something out there, sir," he whispered hoarsely. "Something that don't look quite right to me."

"You've got good eyes, soldier."

Ken Carlie came up behind them. "What is it, sir?" he asked.

"I don't know," said Travis. "We'll wait until the moon rises."

The long minutes dragged past as the moon slowly rose over the eastern heights, gradually silvering the desert.

"Turn out the guard, Mr. Carlie," said Travis. "No noise, mind!"

Carlie turned out the guard. The men stood in the dimness, fingering their rifles, trying to probe the mysterious darkness with their eyes.

"There!" said the sentry. "You see it, sir?"

A hundred yards from the post, right in the center of the Santa Theresa road, a strange growth seemed to have sprouted up since daylight had gone. It was in the shape of a thick cross, some feet higher than a man's head. Travis eyed it until his eyes played tricks on him, but the keen-eyed sentry turned away. "There's a man hanging from that cross," he said in a thick voice.

The moon was higher now, and Travis knew the sentry was right. A man was hanging from the cross. He was naked and his head had been pulled back and lashed to the upright of the cross. The body didn't move.

"Good God," said Ken Carlie.

"Who put it there?" asked a young trooper.

" 'Paches, I'll bet," said a corporal.

The desert was flooding with moonlight, bringing out each detail of the terrain and illuminating the crucified man. There was no sign of human life on the sands nor in the thick brush.

Travis looked at the corporal. "Get a shovel", he said.

The noncom hurried off and was back in a few minutes with the tool. Travis placed a hand on Carlie's shoulder. "Station two men on each roof to cover me. You stay here with two men. Corporal, follow me with two men."

Travis took the shovel in his left hand and drew his Colt with his right. He cocked it and walked out into the open, followed by the three enlisted men. Gun hammers clicked back. Travis' boots made little noise on the soft sand. Now and then he stopped to look and listen, but there was nothing to be seen, and the only sound was the noise of the wind sighing through the brush.

Travis stopped in front of the cross. He looked up into the set face of Amos Corby, the lanky Vermonter whom he had sent out with Troopers John Nolan and Benson Duryea. Amos Corby's sightless eyes stared at the fort.

"No sign of anything," the corporal said huskily.

Travis holstered his Colt and attacked the sand at the base of the cross. The cross tilted as he dug. Travis and the corporal dragged at the cross until it was loose enough to be pulled free from the sand. Corby had been lashed to the cross with rawhide thongs. The corporal cut the tight bonds loose, and they rolled the stiff body to one side. Travis took the corporal's knife and cut through the lashings which held the crossbar to the upright. He carried the two pieces of heavy wood into the brush and hurled the lashings after them. He picked up the body of the courier and walked toward the fort. The three enlisted men walked behind him, holding their weapons at the ready and turning their heads quickly from side to side, waiting for a possible pantherlike rush of Mimbrenos from the brush.

Travis felt a wave of relief pour over him as he passed into the quadrangle. Ken Carlie helped him lower the body to the ground. "Jesus," he said. "Look at the back of his head."

The skull had been smashed by a

murderous blow, but there were no other marks on the naked body. Corby had probably been caught asleep and killed before he had awakened. Travis could visualize what had happened. Corby had made his hidden camp for the day, sure that he was unseen by the Apaches. They had allowed the tired courier time to drop to sleep. Then, at dawn, their favorite time of action in an attack, they had closed in on silent feet to strike hard and sure.

"Christ in the Desert," said an enlisted man.

Travis stood up. "Wrap him in a blanket. Keep him in the guardhouse until daylight. See if you can find an old uniform for him so he can be buried properly, as a soldier."

There was no use telling the enlisted men to forget what they had seen on the road. The gruesome story would be all over the post by morning mess.

Travis walked toward his quarters. He wanted to forget Amos Corby, who had said that his mission was no more dangerous than staying on duty at Fort Joslyn. Travis walked behind his quarters and looked to the east. Somewhere out there the other two couriers might be well on the way to Fort Craig, or they might have suffered the same fate as Corby. But Cuchillo Rojo had played his hand well. The chief was a master at psychological warfare. The real game had just begun, and so far Cuchillo held all the aces.

CHAPTER EIGHT

Morning mess was a quiet affair. None of the officers, with the exception of Major Lester, were very hungry. Everyone knew of the fate of Trooper Corby.

"It is beyond me, Mr. Carlie," said Enos Lester, around a mouthful of bacon, "how your sentries could allow the enemy to approach to within one hundred yards of the post and place the body of Trooper Corby right in the center of the road. Carelessness, Mr. Carlie, pure carelessness. Pass the bread, Mr. Newkirk. I'll thank you for the jam, Mr. DeSantis."

Ken Carlie bit his lip. The major was ready for one of his long and windy diatribes.

The major flourished his fork. "Continual alertness is the only safeguard we have at the present time, Mr. Carlie. You young officers are apt to be lackadaisical in such matters. In my forty years of service I have learned the ways of the red man, but perhaps I forget that you gentlemen are of a different generation, and will not spend the time in learning your business – for, after all, we *are* in a business. I remember one time when I was post quartermaster at Fort Duncan in Texas. The Lipans had been harrying the surrounding countryside, and our post commander, although I hesitate to say so, not being in the habit of criticizing my superior officers as you gentlemen so often do, allowed the garrison to become careless, despite my repeated warnings." Here the major paused to let his words sink in, and also to lay a thick layer of jam on a slice of bread.

The door swung open and Sergeant Ellis appeared. "Sir, there is a messenger here from Santa Theresa."

"We are dining, sergeant."

"I'm sorry, sir, but the man says his message is urgent."

"Bid him enter then," said Lester testily.

A Mexican came into the mess room and took off his steeple hat. He hesitated, looking from one to the other of the officers.

"Speak up, my man," said Lester, turning in his seat. He sank his yellow teeth into his bread and jam and began to chew steadily.

"A woman is missing from the town, Major," the man said, in good English.

"So?"

"It is said she left with her man to try and reach Chihuahua."

"Continue."

"It is thought that they might have been attacked by the Apaches, sir."

Major Lester finished his bread and jam. He wiped his mouth. "What am I to do, sir?"

The man shrugged. "The *alcalde* requests that troops be sent to try and find the woman and her man."

"I have no troops to spare. Is not Captain Cass there in Santa Theresa? That is under his temporary jurisdiction."

The man swallowed. "The captain is not feeling well, Major."

"I am sorry to hear that."

Travis stood up. "I had thought of going into the town to see the progress of the work I ordered done, with your permission, Major Lester."

The major drummed on the table with stubby fingers. "There is work for you here, Captain. However, Santa Theresa is part of my responsibility. Go then and see what you can do."

"I'll take Sergeant Ellis and Baconora with me."

"That will be satisfactory. But no risks, mind! I cannot afford to lose you, Captain Walker."

139

Travis saluted and left the mess. In ten minutes he was on the road with Ellis, Baconora and the Mexican. "The woman must have been loco," opined Baconora.

The Mexican shrugged. "She was headstrong. A fine woman in looks, but headstrong, as I said. Her man did not want to go, but she said she would find a real man to take her if he refused to accompany her. They left last night some time."

"Nice," said Sergeant Ellis. "She'll find some real men among the Mimbrenos, if she lives to talk about it."

The Mexican crossed himself. "Mother of God," he said.

Santa Theresa was quiet under the morning sun. Men and women stood at the corners talking quietly among themselves. "Where are the rest of the soldiers, Captain?" called out an American.

"You have soldiers stationed here," answered Travis.

A man laughed. "Yeah," he said sarcastically.

Travis swung down from his horse and tethered it to the rail in front of James Morris' house. He glanced at the *torreon*. It looked just the same as the last time he had seen it, and the old adobe which he had ordered torn down was still standing as it had been. A surge of anger raced through Travis. Cass had had plenty of time to get the work done.

Travis rapped on the big door. Theresa opened it. There was a worried look on her oval face, but she managed a smile. "It is good to see you," she said.

"Is Captain Cass here, Miss Morris?"

She hesitated. "Yes."

"Please tell him I would like to see him."

"He is in his room. My grandfather insisted that he be quartered here." She led the way down the hall and then out into the patio, a lovely place of blooming flowers and shapely shade trees. A bird sipped at the water in a pool. Theresa stopped at a door. "This is his room," she said.

Travis rapped on the door, but there was no answer. He opened the door and walked inside. He wrinkled his nose at the thick, cloying aura of sweat and sour liquor slops that filled the big room. Charles Cass lay on his belly on the large bed, stripped to his drawers. An empty bottle was on the chair beside the bed. His uniform was scattered across the floor. Travis pulled the door shut behind him. "Cass!" he said.

The big officer did not move.

"Cass! Damn it, wake up, man!"

The officer rolled over and threw an arm

across his eyes. "That you, Dorner?" he said thickly. "Get me some black coffee."

Travis did not answer. He walked to the window and undid the shutters, throwing them back. Sunlight poured into the room. Charles Cass sat up and blinked at Travis. "Oh, it's *you*. What brings you here?"

Travis drew in a breath of fresh air from the open window. "You sleep late, Captain Cass," he said coldly.

Cass reached for a pitcher and poured the water over his touseled blond hair. He hiccupped. "Jesus," he said thickly.

"Did you know a woman and a man of this town left here last night?"

"What am I supposed to do?"

"No one was to leave town. The hills are thick with Apaches."

"I know that."

"Damn it, man, don't you realize what might have happened to them?"

"If they're loco enough to leave town I can't be responsible."

"You don't seem to be responsible for anything! Why haven't you obeyed orders? The *torreon* hasn't been repaired. That old adobe is still standing. I didn't see a work party or a single sentry on the streets."

Cass wiped the water from his face. He looked at Travis with bloodshot eyes. "I only have sixteen men, and those the dregs of the Fort Joslyn garrison – snowbirds, skrimshankers and drunks."

Travis looked at the bottle. "You've been doing a little drinking yourself, Captain."

"I did it off duty."

"You're on duty twenty-four hours a day here until things clear up."

Cass laughed. "Until things clear up? When will that be, Captain Walker?"

"Get dressed. Report to me in ten minutes. I'll issue you orders once more, and by God, Cass, you'd better see to them!"

The big officer stood up. He swayed a little. For a moment Travis thought Cass would rush him. The man was mad clear through. Travis almost hoped he would try it. It would be a pleasure to skin his knuckles on Cass' bristly jaws.

Travis walked outside, shutting the door behind him. Theresa stood by the pool. She was quite a picture as she stood there in the dappled shade, wearing a flaring dress and a thin blouse which exposed her smooth white shoulders. She wore moccasins on her small feet. Travis walked to her. "This is a beautiful and quiet place," he said.

"Yes. Grandfather planned it for my grandmother. She spent her last days here, feeding the birds. They would come to her without fear and flutter about her."

Travis leaned against one of the porch supports. "How is your grandfather?"

"Well enough."

"Who was the woman who left here?"

"Maria Diaz. She once worked for us, but she was wild and flighty. Since that time she took up with Teodoro Vaca. It was she who shamed him into taking her from the town."

"But why?"

Theresa shrugged. "She has relatives in Durango. It was her thought to go to them."

"Didn't she realize that the Apaches are watching the town?"

"Teodoro has traveled much. It is said he meant to travel at night and hide during the day. But it is a long way to Durango. A way of peril. Pray to God that she is safe."

Travis looked away. "The odds are against it, Theresa."

"Yes . . . I know. I liked her. She was so pretty and popular. If Teodoro had not taken her she would have talked some other fool into doing so."

"How old was she?"

"Nineteen, captain. There was no one in Santa Theresa who could dance like her, and she sang like a bird."

"The soldiers have not worked here?"

She shook her dark head.

"They have been drinking?"

"I don't want to talk about it, Captain."

"It doesn't matter. I know."

She looked across the sunlit patio at Charles Cass' door. "I do not like him," she said.

"Has he bothered you?"

She looked away. "No," she said quietly.

Travis knew she was lying. Charlie Cass wasn't the type of man who would be around Theresa Morris, or any other good-looking young woman, without trying his hand at her. Cass had been made an officer by Act of Congress, but they hadn't been able to make him a gentleman, in the smallest sense of the word, by legislation. Evelyn Cass was a fit mate for her husband. Travis wondered how the two of them had ever mated.

Cass opened his door and walked out into the sunlight. The bright rays must have lanced deep into his throbbing skull, because he winced and pulled down his hat-brim.

Travis looked at the girl. "I'll see what I can do about Maria and Teodoro," he said.

Charles Cass smiled sarcastically. "All we've got here is two squads of infantry," he said. "You figure on chasing out into the desert with them?"

Travis turned quickly. "No. Your job is to get to work on the details I outlined for you. I'll go after those two."

Cass smiled again. "Do," he said dryly. He looked at Theresa, not missing those of her charms he could see, and mentally stripping her to view the rest of her charms in his mind's eye. The man was a born lecher, thought Travis.

"There is breakfast for you, Captain Cass," said Theresa.

"Forget it," said Travis. "Come with me, Cass."

"I haven't eaten yet."

"You've got all day."

"You have no right..." The officer's voice trailed off as he saw the icy look in Travis' eyes.

"Come on!"

Theresa led the way into the house and up the long hallway to the door. Cass wet his lips as he looked at her hips. He glanced at Travis, and then looked away. There was a sly grin on his flushed face.

"Good morning, Theresa," said Travis.

"You will come back to have coffee with Grandfather?"

"Perhaps. I want to see if I can find Maria."

The big door closed behind the two officers. "A nice bit of fluff," said Cass as he glanced back at the door. "Mixed blood seems to make them prettier and develops them earlier."

"So? You're an expert on the subject?"

Cass grinned. "I've been around," he said.

"You'd better get around this town. Hop to it. I'm going out into the desert."

Cass nodded. He watched Travis mount his horse. Travis was followed by Sergeant Ellis, Baconora and the Mexican who had come to Fort Joslyn. "You ramrod-backed son of a bitch," said Cass aloud. "I hope Cuchillo nails you good."

Jorge, the Mexican, drew rein just short of the low foothills and looked back at Travis. "They rode burros," he said. "We know this because they were missing from the corral of Señor Morris."

Baconora cast about, riding slowly, with his eyes fixed on the ground. He waved them on. "Here," he said. "Two burros crossed this wash." He swung down and raked quick fingers through some droppings. "Fresh. Not more than eight hours old." He wiped his hands on the seat of his filthy trousers.

Sergeant Ellis nodded. "Damned fools," he said.

They went on. The hills were quiet, brooding in the late morning sun. "Look," said Jorge quickly.

High overhead three *zopilotes*, the great

land buzzards of the Southwest, wheeled like scraps of charred paper caught in an updraft. Lower and lower they swung, until they passed beyond a cone-shaped hill.

The four men did not talk as they rode toward the hill, but carbines were placed across thighs and Colts were loosened in their sheaths.

The obscene birds rose heavily and reluctantly from the brush as they heard the approach of the horses. The four men drew rein and looked about from beneath their hat-brims. There was no sign of Apaches, but right in front of them, in the soft sand, were the marks of many horses' hoofs. To one side lay a rusty *escopeta*, which had evidently been smashed over a rock. "Teodoro's, I think," said Jorge softly.

Farther on, they saw a steeple hat lying beneath a clump of mesquite. Travis held up an arm. They dismounted and led their horses forward through the tangled mess of brush and shattered rocks. The sun beat down on them like the heat from a baker's oven.

"Look," said Sergeant Ellis.

The man had been roped to an upright finger of rock. The sun shone on his naked body. They had had their fun with Teodoro Vaca before he had been allowed the blessedness of death. Knives had changed

148

him from the likeness of God into something indescribably horrid. Only his face had not been touched, but his staring, sightless eyes still mirrored the horrors he had seen and experienced.

"Christ," said Ellis.

Baconora spat. "There she is," he said, without emotion.

Maria Diaz would never dance and sing again for the *bravos* of Santa Theresa, nor anyone else. Teodoro Vaca had probably seen what had happened to his lady love, and his mind might have snapped at the sight. At least Travis hoped it had, for the foulness of the thing would have cracked most men's minds.

Her pitiful rags of finery had been ripped from her body as she fought a hopeless fight with nails and feet against her assaulters. Sergeant Ellis took a blanket from his cantle and threw it over the poor relic which lay on the hot sands, with broken-nailed fingers dug deep into the earth in final agony.

Baconora spat out his wad of sweet chewing tobacco and cut another chew. "Must'a been at least seven or eight of 'em," he said. He stowed the fresh wad into his mouth and began to work it into pliability.

Jorge crossed himself. "She was like a bird," he said softly, "always singing and fluttering about."

149

"Cut Teodoro loose," said Travis. "Let's get out of here!"

They placed the bodies on horses and lashed them into position. "Might just as well have left them out here," said the scout. He looked up at the wheeling *zopilotes*. "Them boys would soon take care of them," he said.

"Mother of Jesus!" said Jorge. "Have you no feelings?"

"Coldblooded bastard," said Mack Ellis.

There were tears in Jorge's brown eyes as he drew the blanket down about Maria. "There was a time," he said brokenly, "when she almost became my wife. It was months ago. I did not have enough money."

"Forget it, my friend," said Travis quietly.

They rode slowly toward the road. The *zopilotes* followed them for a time, and then flew off in search of other prey.

They buried them in a common grave in the little walled cemetery of Santa Theresa, and most of the townspeople were there. They knew now that there was no chance for any of them to escape. They were in a prison without bars, with the executioners biding their time in the hazy hills.

Captain Cass had his men working on the *torreon*, aided by some of the men of the town, while others had started the task of leveling the old adobe. Two-wheeled *carretas* creaked and groaned between the spring and the various cisterns in town, filling them to capacity. A corporal, helped by one of his squad, worked on the shabby weapons of the townspeople. Several women had been assigned to rolling cartridges, under the direction of a trooper. Another corporal had formed some of the able-bodied men of the town into a volunteer militia, to augment the small force commanded by Charles Cass.

Sergeant Ellis was a tower of strength to Travis. The big noncom rawhided the men who tried to shirk, and under the whiplash of his tongue the work progressed swiftly. But Captain Cass kept away from Travis. He stood in the meager shade of the *torreon*, puffing at a cigar, while his head pounded like an Apache tom-tom.

A servant came from the house of James Morris to invite Travis for dinner. Travis was in no hurry to get back to Fort Joslyn and under the thumb of Enos Lester, so he accepted the invitation. He sent Baconora and Sergeant Ellis back to the post in the middle of the afternoon.

A velvety dusk settled over the great valley, and candlelight shone through the cracks in the shutters of Santa Theresa. The *torreon* had been reënforced as well as it could be, and the old adobe was leveled. Sentries, both civilian and military, paced the dark streets of the little *placita*. Travis cleaned up in the back room of Jonas Simpson's *cantina* and then stopped at the bar for a drink.

Jonas Simpson eyed Travis with his one good eye. It had a strange effect, as though the one good eye had much more penetrating power than two good ones. "You think all your preparations will do any good for us, Captain?" he asked.

Travis shrugged. "We do the best we can," he said.

Jonas nodded. "Yeah ... *you* did. All that bastard Cass did was sit around and swill *aguardiente*, with both eyes peeled for a likely looking woman. Well, he run off the best of the lot. You saw what happened to her."

Travis straightened up. "What do you mean?"

"You mean you didn't hear about it? Hell, it's common gossip that Cass was after Maria Diaz. He was trying to run the town like one of them feudal lords, or whatever you call 'em. Maria was scared to death of him. She talks that poor lovesick Teodoro into going with her. He was more scairt than she was, but he goes. You know the rest."

Travis emptied his glass. "Just what did Cass do to Maria?"

"Well, she was helping out a little at the Morris *casa* to make a little money. Cass traps her one day in his room. It was old Angelique who hears her. From what she said, Cass was really giving Maria a going over, and Angelique got there just in time. It wasn't until she threatened to tell the *alcalde* that Cass let the girl go. By that time he had had his way with her. Chihuahua! There's a lot of the beast in that man."

Travis refilled his glass. A picture formed in his mind – the sight of Maria Diaz lying out there under the hot sun, ravaged and torn by the tigers of the human species under the tortured eyes of her Teodoro. He tightened his right hand. Suddenly the glass shattered in his grip, and he felt a sharp sensation of pain. *Aguardiente* and blood trickled from his hand as he opened it.

"*Jesusita!*" said Simpson.

Travis let the broken glass drop to the sanded floor. He bound his handkerchief about the hand and drew the knot tight with his teeth. Jonas Simpson looked at Travis' eyes, then looked quickly away, for he did not like what he saw there.

"Maybe I talk too much," said Jonas.

"No. Just enough."

Jonas wiped the bar. "I got a feelin' you aim to have a talk with Charlie Cass."

"I will."

The *cantina* owner looked up. "I ain't no angel. I got one foot in hell and the other on a pool of grease, but I don't like Charlie Cass and I did like Maria. Oh, she was a little wild at times, but she was no *puta*. She would have settled down and made a good wife and mother. This I know. I never heard of any man making her in this *placita*, and there ain't much I miss around here. I'll bet my *cantina* against that hat of yours that Charlie Cass was the first man who got her."

Travis walked to the door. "He wasn't the last. There were at least eight or nine Mimbrenos in at the death, and it wasn't a quick, clean death, Jonas. Good night."

Jonas Simpson wiped the sweat from his bald head. "God help Good-time Charlie Cass when that cold-eyed bastard Travis Walker reckons with him."

Travis lit a half of a cigar he had been saving and leaned against the base of the *torreon*. Now and then he saw the shadowy figure of a sentry pace along the plaza. The night wind swept in from the cooling desert, bringing with it the mingled odors of sage and mesquite. Here and there in the dark blue blanket of the sky an

154

ice-chip star winked forth. The faint cry of a coyote drifted to him from the hills.

A slim young woman appeared around the *torreon*. "The *capitán* is lonely this night?" she asked softly.

"No."

She sidled up to him. "I am."

"Go home, little one."

"Do you not like me?"

"I do not know you."

"I am Rafaela."

"It is a pretty name."

"Do I not have more than the pretty name?"

"You are very pretty, Rafaela."

"Come with me then."

"I dine with the *alcalde* tonight."

She laughed. "You will get nothing from Saint Theresa."

"Close your beak, little bird."

She leaned back against the warm wall of the tower. "My house is the second one beyond this tower. The *capitán* with the yellow hair has already been with me. Ask him. He will tell you of my charms."

"I'm sure he can."

She laughed again. "What a bull that one is. But I do not sleep with the common soldiers – only the officers."

"A real lady," said Travis dryly.

155

"You will come then later tonight? I will wait."

"No."

"Before God!" she said angrily. "Are you a man of stone?"

He shook his head and looked down at her. "I was the man who brought in the bodies of Maria and Teodoro. Did you see Maria, Rafaela?"

She shivered. "I did not, but I have heard of what happened to her."

"Now you know why I will not come. Good night, Rafaela."

"Good night, *capitán*."

She vanished silently into the darkness. The odor of her cheap perfume seemed to spoil the taste of his cigar. He hurled it to the ground and walked toward the big house of James Morris.

It was Angelique who admitted Travis. She started to usher him into the house, but he took her by the arm and drew her outside. "What is this I hear about Captain Cass and Maria?" he asked.

"It was a terrible thing. She was to help me here in the house. I sent her to make the captain's bed. I did not know he was still in it. Miss Theresa was shopping, and the *alcalde* was in his study. He cannot hear too well. Only Esteban was in the house, and he

156

is old and cannot hear at all. I heard Maria scream and hurried to the room." She stopped and looked away.

"Go on!" he said fiercely.

"It was terrible, *capitán*. He is like the mad bull with a woman. She was such a child. He threw me aside, but I am strong and came right back. He was going to strike me when I told him I would tell the *alcalde*. Then he laughed and told me to get her out of the house. He threw money at us as we left. I am afraid of him, and I am afraid for Miss Theresa with him in the house."

"Don't worry about her."

She slid a hand inside her dress and drew out a slim-bladed *cuchillo*. "He will not touch her while I am here, *capitán*."

They went into the house, and she led him to the dining room. James Morris sat in his great chair. Theresa sat near the fireplace. She wore a black dress trimmed with exquisite lace. There was a comb in her dark hair, and she had drawn a filmy mantilla over it. It covered her bare shoulders, but their whiteness could be seen through the fine mesh of the lace. Travis' breath seemed to catch in his throat. She could have been sitting there waiting for one of the great masters to paint her in immortal oils.

The huge table was spread with a heavy

157

white cloth, and the candlelight glistened softly on the heavy service. James Morris was evidently a man of great wealth.

"Good evening, *alcalde*," said Travis.

"Good evening to you, Captain Walker."

Theresa came forward. "You have hurt your hand," she exclaimed.

Travis nodded. There seemed to be more than just concern for an injured friend in her low voice. "It is nothing," he said.

"She has some skill in such matters," said the major. "Let her examine it."

Travis smiled. "Before dinner?"

"She is strong, Captain, much as my wife was."

Theresa took Travis' bandaged hand in her soft ones. She removed the bandage. "It must be disinfected," she said. "How did you do it?"

"A glass broke in my hand."

Her dark eyes studied him. "It must have broken very hard to inflict such cuts."

"Yes."

"Come with me, Captain."

She led the way into another room and took out bandages and antiseptic from a cabinet. She poured water into a basin, then bathed the wound. He winced a little as she applied the carbolic. She bandaged the hand swiftly and neatly.

158

He looked down at her dark hair and at the smooth white shoulders, now exposed where her mantilla had fallen back, and there was a great desire within him to pass his free hand across the delightful flesh. She looked up at him, and there was an odd look in her eyes as though she had read his mind. But she did not release his hand.

"*Gracias,*" he said.

"You must be more careful, Captain."

"The name is Travis, Theresa."

"Travis, then."

Her tone of voice broke the halter on Travis' restraint. He drew her close, and she made no effort to pull away. He tilted back her head and kissed her softly. For a moment she hesitated, and then she slid an arm about his neck and drew him close, kissing him again and again. Then she broke away, passed a hand across her mouth and walked quickly to the door. "Grandfather will wonder what has become of us," she said.

"I'm wondering what will become of us."

Her dark eyes held his. "I think I know," she said, and then she was gone.

Travis touched the bandage. He had thought he had been in love before. He had known many women of all kinds, and bore the invisible scars of what he thought had been lost loves on his soul, but now he knew for sure he had never really been in love as he was now.

Travis entered the great room. Theresa stood beside her grandfather as before, but there was a difference in her now as she looked at Travis.

Angelique bustled in to serve the meal, aided by aged Esteban. The door swung open and Charles Cass came in. "You might as well set four places, Angelique," he said.

The serving woman shot him a look of hate, then looked at Theresa. Theresa looked away, but her grandfather spoke up. "Captain Cass, is it not? You are welcome, sir."

Cass had been drinking again. He lounged over to the sideboard and helped himself to a glass of wine. Travis clenched his hands so hard his right hand began to bleed afresh. Theresa shook her head at him and then looked down at James Morris. Travis nodded. He helped her push the old man's chair up to the head of the table. Cass emptied his glass and filled it again. "You have a way of getting things done, Walker," he said.

"Thanks."

"Don't mention it. You've got a great future in the service – if you live to see it."

Theresa flushed. James Morris looked toward Cass. "You sound melancholy, Captain Cass," he said quietly.

"These are melancholy times, sir."

"I agree, but we will survive them as we have so many others."

"I hope so."

The dinner was good, and conversation was at a minimum. Now and then, Travis dared to look deep into Theresa's eyes to read the message he wanted to read again and again. After a time Charles Cass began to notice the two of them. It must be damned apparent, thought Travis.

Cass drank steadily, spending more time with the bottle than he did with the food. After a time his eyes darted again and again to study Theresa, particularly where the cleft of her firm breasts showed in her low-cut bodice. Travis suddenly lost his appetite. The man was an outright lecher.

Angelique served coffee and liqueurs after the meal. Charlie Cass drank everything placed in front of him, with frequent trips to the sideboard and his speech became thicker. Only the aged major didn't seem to notice anything out of the ordinary, but Travis felt sure that James Morris knew that the officer was getting drunk.

Finally Travis could stand no more. "I'd like to talk to you privately, Cass," he said quietly.

The captain emptied his glass. "We're with

friends, Walker," he said. "They can hear anything you have to say."

"I'd rather speak with you alone."

"I'm not through here yet."

Travis felt a growing rage, but he did not dare show it. Impulse demanded that he cross the room and drag the big man outside, but cold reason bridled his anger.

James Morris yawned slightly. "It is getting late," he said.

Cass refilled his glass. "Maybe Captain Walker would like to speak with Miss Morris alone, too," he suggested.

"What do you mean, sir?" asked the *alcalde*.

Cass grinned. "Anyone who has eyes can see what I mean, *alcalde*."

The old man looked toward Travis. "I don't understand him, sir."

Travis stood up. "Captain Cass has been drinking. His duties have him worried, and he is trying to relax."

Cass laughed loudly. "By God, that's good, Walker! I didn't think you had a sense of humor at all."

"What does this man mean, sir?" persisted Morris.

Theresa placed a hand on the old man's shoulder. "Please don't excite yourself."

"What is going on here?"

Travis looked Cass full in the eye. "Excuse yourself," he said coldly. "I'll see you in the patio."

Charlie Cass wanted to show Theresa he wasn't afraid of Travis; he wanted to show her so badly it hurt deep inside, but the cold rage in Travis' eyes was too much for even him. He bowed to Theresa. "Good night, Miss Morris. Good night, Major Morris." He weaved a little as he walked toward the door. He turned as he opened it, eyed Theresa and Travis, then left the room. His laugh came back to them.

James Morris looked toward Travis, "Well, sir!"

Theresa slid an arm about the old man's gnarled neck. "It is very simple, Grandfather. I am in love with Captain Walker and he is in love with me."

"Mother of God!"

"It's true, sir," said Travis quietly.

Morris raised his heavy cane and shook it. "You come to Santa Theresa to help us, and you connive behind my back to delude this child into such things. If I could stand up, sir, I'd thrash you. If I could see I would invite you out."

Theresa took the cane from his big hands. "How old was Grandmother when you married her?"

"What has that to do with it?"

163

"*How old*, Grandfather?"

"Eighteen."

"She was *sixteen*, Grandfather. I remember the stories you used to tell of eloping with her and how her three brothers pursued you for two days and how she rode like a *vaquero* beside you, never complaining, until you were safe."

"That was long ago. Such things are not done now."

"My mother was but eighteen when your own son married her. It is said you raised hell, to use the proper term, because my mother didn't meet your requirements for a daughter-in-law."

"She was but a child!"

Theresa shook her pretty head. "That was not the reason at all. It was because she was not Anglo, nor even of pure Spanish blood. She was half Opata and proud of it, but you didn't like the thought of mixed blood in the family."

The old man bowed his head. She had struck home. "I'm sorry about that, Granddaughter. It was long ago. I have learned a great deal of tolerance since those days. You are all I have left, and are as dear to me as my son was. You must forgive an old man, Theresa, and you too, Captain Walker."

"Forget it, sir."

The sightless eyes raised to look directly at Travis, and he again had the feeling that the old man could see him plainly. "My grand-daughter is not the type of frontier woman who will throw herself at a man. Did you approach her first, sir?"

Travis looked at the young woman. She nodded. Travis came closer to the old man. "I think it was mutual, sir."

"You'll marry her then?"

"No."

"What do you mean, sir! *What do you mean?*"

"There is a war on us, sir. Fort Joslyn and Santa Theresa are in desperate straits. I'm a soldier on duty here. The odds are high against us, there's no use in deluding you on that point. If we survive this mess I intend to ask Theresa to be my wife."

Her eyes held his as though she'd never let him go.

The old man nodded. "You are a man of honor, Captain Walker. But I must request you to see Theresa only by our customs. With her *duenna,* and only when I give permission."

"Agreed."

Theresa laughed softly. "But, Grandfather, I have no *duenna.*"

"Angelique will serve as such." The old man held out his right hand and Travis

165

gripped it. "Go now, Captain," said James Morris. "I wish to speak privately with Theresa."

Travis touched her cheek with his left hand, then walked to the door. He turned to look at her, and then he left the room.

Charlie Cass was in the patio, leaning against an upright. Travis walked to him. "You certainly conducted yourself like a damned fool in there," he said.

"Save the lecture."

"As your senior officer I request you to conduct yourself like an officer and a gentleman."

Cass yawned. "There's a helluva lot of seniority between us, Walker. Get off your high horse."

"I'm warning you just once."

"You come in out of the desert from where God alone knows. You bull Enos Lester into thinking you're something special. You move in on the old man in there and make him think you're the Angel Gabriel came to save his God-damned two-bit *placita*. Then you grab off his granddaughter. How was it, Walker? Worth the effort?"

Travis swung his left hand and the hard open palm snapped the officer's head back against the post. Cass raised his right hand to his stinging face, then dropped it to his

166

gun butt. "You like your whores high class, eh, Walker?"

Travis closed his injured right hand and hit Cass neatly on the jaw. The big man went down hard, groveling on the tiles. Travis stood over him. "I warned you," he said thinly. "Now listen to me again – you'll do your duty here as a soldier. If you so much as bother Theresa I'll hunt you down and kill you." He turned on a heel and walked toward the hallway.

Cass gripped his Colt butt. "You'll pay for this," he yelled. Travis disappeared from sight. Cass pulled himself to his feet. "By God, you'll pay for it, you brass-bound son of a bitch," he said quietly.

Travis walked toward the outer door. Theresa stepped from her room and looked up at him. He drew her close and kissed her. She laughed softly. "My *duenna* isn't here," she protested.

Travis raised her head. "There's one thing I haven't said to you yet. I love you, Theresa Morris, with all my heart and soul. Somehow I'll take you away from here."

"I know that," she said simply. "I seemed to know it the first time I saw you."

When Travis was out into the moonlit plaza he wondered at the mystery of it all. He had found the woman he loved – the only woman

167

he would ever love. He had made a deadly enemy of Charles Cass, a man who would never forget what Travis had done to smash his superego.

CHAPTER NINE

The moon was up high as Travis rode the Santa Theresa – Fort Joslyn road. Now and then he drew rein to sit his saddle and listen to the night sounds. The Apaches rarely attacked at night, but a bold warrior, safe in ambush, might risk a sure killing shot to get a lone rider.

He was a mile from the fort when he turned his horse aside to enter the brush. If the Mimbrenos were watching the post, they would keep warriors along the moonlit road to guard the approaches.

He was a quarter of a mile from the fort when he saw the moonlight glistening on something in a clearing. It lay on a low mound of sand from which the tussocks had been pulled away and cast in a pile to one side. Travis dismounted and led his horse toward the mound. Then he stopped short. What he saw was a complete skeleton, the moonbeams shining on the creamy-yellow bones. Beside the ankle and wrist bones he saw pegs driven into the sand, with rawhide thongs lying loosely about the wrists and ankles, or at least where they had been.

Travis dropped the reins and drew his Sharps free from the saddle. He cocked and capped it, then moved to the base of the low mound, not ten feet from the grisly relic of a man. Tiny black objects moved busily about the skeleton. Sonoran ants, black, venomous and voracious. He had not known they existed in the deserts of New Mexico, but he had seen them in the Sonoran deserts in the country of the fierce and predatory Yaquis, blood cousins to the equally vicious Apaches.

The man had been stripped and bound over the ant mound. There was no telling who or what he had been. The ants could strip the flesh from a man in twelve hours, because they worked busily by day and night. Travis ascended the mound and looked about. There was no sign of life. He drew his knife out and cut away the loose rawhide thongs. As he did so one of the ants got at his left hand. It was like the jabbing of a hatpin almost to the bone. He jerked back his hand, feeling the quick poison of the voracious insect burning in his blood.

Travis slid down the slope. He glanced back

at the skeleton. The ants were cleaning up the last fragments of flesh. Only the gristle ligaments would be left by dawn, holding the bones together. In time the bones would turn white and drop away from each other as the ligaments rotted apart.

Then he saw the battered hat hanging from a mesquite branch. It was a Kossuth hat such as he wore, but it had been an enlisted man's headgear, as he could tell by the quality of the wool and the half inch ribbed grosgrain ribbon, originally black, which had faded to a funereal purple from exposure to the elements. Travis turned the hat upside down and turned down the wide leather sweatband. The name J. Nolan had been lettered inside the band.

Travis glanced at the remains of John Nolan, the quiet Pennsylvanian. He had said that he was sick of waiting for Cuchillo Rojo to swoop down on Fort Joslyn.

"Two gone and one to go," said Travis aloud. Corby and Nolan had never made Fort Craig. That left Benson Duryea, the courier who had been ordered by Travis to go the long way around to Fort Craig. Where was he? Would he show up as Corby and Nolan had done? Cuchillo Rojo had made sure that Nolan would be identified, by leaving the dead trooper's hat near his remains.

Travis mounted and rode toward the fort, with his carbine across his thighs and Nolan's hat hooked to his belt.

The moon shone on the adobe walls of the fort. There was a sentry standing just beyond the gate. "Halt! Who goes there?"

"Officer of the garrison!"

"Advance to be recognized!"

Travis raised his hand and spurred the horse forward.

The sentry lowered his rifle, "Captain Walker! The captain is taking his life in his hands riding in the desert alone."

Travis swung down. "How has it been?"

"Quiet, sir. Too damned quiet."

"Any sign of the Apaches?"

"A little smoke in the hills."

Travis nodded. He led his horse past the sentry into the moonlit quadrangle. Sergeant Ellis appeared. "I'll take your horse, sir. The major wishes to see you. He left orders you were to report to him in his quarters as soon as you returned."

"Thanks, Ellis."

"Everything all right in town, sir?"

"As well as can be expected."

"I gave those two corporals a little living hell about their laxity before I left, sir."

"You can't put all the blame on them."

"What does the captain mean?"

"Nothing. Ellis, I have a job for you tonight."

"Yes, sir?"

"Half a mile from here, on the east side of the road, you'll find all that's left of John Nolan."

"Jesus!" blurted Ellis. "Him too?"

"Him too."

Ellis shook his head. "Poor Johnny. I thought he'd make it if any of us could. What about Duryea?"

"I don't know, Sergeant. Take two or three good men. Go and get Nolan. Don't let anyone see him as he is."

"Is it that bad?"

"Yes," said Travis quietly. "Wrap him in canvas and sew it up. A saddler can do it. I want no one to see him as he is. You understand?"

"Yes, sir."

"Wrap him up yourself and then bring him back. You will not say that it is Nolan. Just an unidentified body."

"I understand, sir."

"Keep your mouth shut."

"Certainly, Captain!"

Travis handed Ellis the Kossuth hat. "Bury that with what you find."

Travis walked toward the major's quarters. Ellis watched him, then looked down at the hat. "Poor Johnny," he said. He led the horse to the corral.

Major Lester was wrapped in a blanket and seated in a chair. He looked up as Travis entered the stifling room. The fire snapped and crackled in the big fireplace, filling the room with the resinous odors of mesquite wood. "Good to see you, Walker," he said. "How did it go?"

"The woman and her companion were murdered by the Apaches."

Enos Lester paled. "They left the town?"

"Yes."

"The fools!"

"They had a reason. But they paid for their foolishness."

Lester drew his blanket tightly about his shoulders and shivered a little. "The defenses of the town are all right?"

"As well as can be expected. I don't think Cuchillo will make an open attack on Santa Theresa, but he'll probably make nuisance raids."

"I'm sure Captain Cass is doing it all right there."

"He is," said Travis dryly. There was no use in complaining about Charles Cass. There was no one else to replace him. Travis hoped his treatment of the drunken fool would straighten him out, but he had little faith in the thought.

"Let us hope our two remaining couriers will get through. It is a terrible responsibility for a sick man here, Captain Walker."

Travis nodded. "I know, sir. I'll give you all the support I am able to. But you must know that Trooper Nolan is dead."

Lester swallowed quickly. "That leaves Duryea to carry the dispatches."

"Yes."

"What happened to Nolan?"

There was no use in telling the gruesome details to the shaken man in front of him, thought Travis. "I found his body half a mile from the fort, sir."

Enos Lester plucked at his lower lip. "I had no faith in sending those men, sir! You practically overruled me on that, Captain! *You* sent those men to a sure death!"

Travis did not answer. He knew Lester wasn't through castigating him.

"In forty years of service, sir, I have developed a foresight into such matters. All you have done is to weaken the garrison still further. It was your idea to garrison Santa Theresa and weaken us still beyond that point. Now we have other troubles. Someone on this post is trying to incite some of the enlisted men to desert and join the Confederacy. I assure you, sir, that man will be shot as a traitor if I can find him."

"You're sure about this, sir?"

"Certainly!" snapped the major. "I have not manufactured the rumor out of whole cloth! My orderly, Private Kelligan, reported it to me."

"Where did he hear such a tale?"

"It is being talked about in the enlisted men's mess, but no one has mentioned the culprit's name. I want you to investigate, sir! If you identify the man he must be court-martialed."

"Yes, sir."

Lester waved a pudgy hand. "I am surrounded by fools and traitors. Beset by the Apaches. Sick in body but not sick in heart. I am a soldier, sir!"

"I know, Major."

Lester leaned forward. "I suppose you think we should abandon the fort and strike for the Rio Grande?"

"I mentioned that once before, sir."

"Do you think it could be done?"

"It's possible yet, Major."

"Tell me how?"

"But your orders say that you must remain here until ordered otherwise."

The major looked away. "Well, it might be left to my discretion. If it was, and, mind, I'm not saying it is so, how would you perform the evacuation?"

Travis eyed the old man. He was in a hell of a nervous condition for sure. "I'd strip the command down to fighting gear, carrying nothing but rations and all the ammunition we have on hand. I'd take just enough wagons to transport rations, ammunition, women and children. The infantry could march with the wagon train while the cavalry, under my command, could fend off Apache attacks. The Apaches don't like to attack steady infantry. In some cases the Indians are more afraid of infantry fire than they are of cavalry attack. We could strike for the road to the Rio Grande and fight our way through."

"And supposing we met a strong force of Confederates if we got past the Apaches?"

"Why, sir, we'd have to surrender and take the fortunes of war."

Lester flushed. "That would end my career of forty years of loyal service. I would be put on half pay if I was to be paroled."

The old man was a downright fool, thought Travis.

Enos Lester pounded the arm of his chair. "Was ever commanding officer put into such straits?"

"I imagine similar circumstances have beset commanding officers before, sir."

Lester shook his head. "Forty loyal years. Did the Commanding officer of the Department of New Mexico think of that? Did he care about me? Not at all, sir. Not at all. I will not go home on half pay, discarded like a condemned mule, to face my people and make excuses for the remainder of my life. I will not have it!"

Travis eyed the frightened old man. He was more concerned about his damned reputation, *if* he had any at all, than he was about the lives of the people who depended on him for protection.

"Let me alone," said Lester quietly. "Find the man who is a traitor. Oh, I'll crucify him!"

Travis left the stifling room. He remembered the talk he had had with Martin Newkirk. There had been something in Newkirk's tone when he had suggested that Lester's orders could not include Travis. Travis meant to pry specific information out of Newkirk.

Travis walked toward his quarters. Lester wanted him to locate the traitor who was supposedly inciting the enlisted men into deserting the army to join the Confederacy. There were mostly Northerners among the enlisted men, with a leavening of Border States' and Southern States' men. One of the latter two types might be responsible, but it wouldn't be easy singling out the culprit.

The door of the infantrymen's quarters hung open. The thin music of a fife drifted out into the night, backed by the soft beating of a drum. Travis stopped to listen. It was a moment before he recognized the tune. It was *The White Cockade*. Travis slowly walked to the door and looked inside. A grizzled corporal sat on a stool near the door, tootling his fife, while a young infantryman rattled away on the drum. The fifer stopped as he saw Travis and slowly lowered his instrument, while the drummer played on and then stopped in the middle of a roll.

The corporal stood up. "Attention!" he roared.

The men tumbled from their cots and stood at attention.

"As you were," said Travis.

"Maybe we were making too much noise, sir?" said the corporal.

"No," said Travis. "Was that *The White Cockade?*"

The fifer grinned. "It was, sir. A fine tune, is it not?"

"It's been a long time since I've heard it. I always liked fife and drum music."

"I'm Corporal Stewart, sir. B. Comapny."

"How many years' service?"

The man drew himself up. "Twenty years, sir."

"You were in the Mexican War?"

"I was, sir. Fourth Infantry."

"Come outside a moment."

Stewart followed Travis outside. "Yes, sir?"

"What part of the country are you from, Stewart?"

"New Jersey, sir. But I was born and raised in Massachusetts."

"A real Yankee, eh?"

"I'm proud of it, sir."

"I'm sure you are." Travis walked away from the barracks. He turned. "You know the men of your company pretty well?"

"I've been with most of them over two years, Captain."

"Have you heard any talk about deserting and joining the Confederacy?"

Stewart flushed a little. "Well . . ."

"Speak up!"

"Well, sir, there has been talk about it."

"Who started it?"

"I don't know, sir."

Travis nodded. "You don't know or you won't say?"

"Let's put it this way, Captain Walker – if I had heard any such talk I would have lambasted the man who said it. All I've heard are rumors."

Travis rubbed his jaw. "I haven't any doubt about your loyalty, Stewart. Keep your ears open and let me know if you can find out who the man is, because as sure as I'm standing here, there has been such talk."

"It hasn't come from my squad, sir, nor from my company. In fact I don't know of any enlisted man who has been talking such tripe."

"Thanks."

Stewart hesitated. "I don't know for sure about the officers though, sir."

"What do you mean?"

The old soldier fingered his battered fife. "If you're looking for such a man, sir, you'd better look twice at some of the officers."

"Who?"

"I'd rather not say, Captain, because I ain't sure."

"Thanks. Go back to your quarters."

"You want us to stop playing, sir?"

"Stop at *Tattoo*."

"Right, sir." The noncom saluted and returned to his barracks. A moment later Travis heard him speak. "All right, Billy, let's try *Hell on the Wabash*."

"What did the captain want to talk to you about?"

"My fifing. He wants to hear *Hell on the Wabash*. Let's go! One! Two! Three!"

The reedy music started in again, with the soft beat of the drum underlying the tune. Travis shrugged.

Someone moved from behind a wagon. It was Maggie Gillis. "You've been away, Captain. We've missed you."

Travis smiled. "Who has? Ben Joad?"

She laughed. "Ben ain't been feeling too chipper since you marked his ugly face."

"I was sorry for that."

"I'm not. I hate him."

"Now, Maggie!"

She came close to him. "Watch him, Captain. He don't never forget things like that."

"I'll watch him," promised Travis.

She looked at the barracks. "I heard what you asked Sam Stewart."

"So?"

"He was right. It ain't no enlisted man who's been talking about treason."

"Go on."

"It's an officer."

"Who?"

"You won't say it was me who talked?"

"I'll keep your secret."

"It was Mr. Carlie."

"You're sure?"

181

"As sure as I'm Maggie Gillis."

"I see. Tell me about it."

She looked about and then came closer. "I was sleeping in the wagon, one night, where it was cooler. Mr. Carlie was officer of the guard. He came by the wagon, and some of the enlisted men was sitting outside the barracks chewing the fat. They was talking about the war, and one of them said he was from Tennessee and didn't want to go East. He said he'd rather fight Apaches than Confederates.

"Another one agreed with the first one who talked. Then Mr. Carlie began to talk about it, saying he wasn't so sure the Federal government had any right to fight against the South, because they was only sticking up for States' Rights, which he believed in.

"They got into quite a palaver about the whole thing. Mr. Carlie said a man had a right to forget his oath of allegiance to the Federal government, for anyone who gave his oath gave it to the whole country, not just to the North."

Travis nodded. "Thanks, Maggie."

"You said you wouldn't say who told you."

"I won't."

Corporal Stewart was now playing *Peas Upon a Trencher*. Maggie turned her head. "Pretty, ain't it? I like music. Do you?"

182

"Yes."

"Will we leave here soon, Captain?"

"I don't know. I wish we would."

"You'll make sure I go with you?"

"Yes. Good night, Maggie."

"Good night, Captain."

Travis turned to go. She pulled his arm. "Some time, Captain, will you come and talk with me?"

He turned and looked down at her piquant face, half that of a woman and half that of a girl. He raised her chin and kissed her. "Maybe, Maggie. We'll see."

She looked after him as he walked. "A real gentleman," she said softly. There was a suspicious glinting in her big eyes.

Corporal Stewart raised his voice. "Damn it, Billy! You're off half a beat most of the time! Let's try *The Wrecker's Daughter,* and mind you get the time!"

Travis walked to his quarters and went in. Clint Vaughn was seated at his desk. He looked up as Travis entered. "Welcome home," he said.

"Thanks."

"You've got an odd look on your *cara.*"

Travis dropped on his bunk. "What do you know about Ken Carlie?"

"He's a better officer than any of them here, you excepted."

183

"*Gracias.*"

"Why do you ask?"

Travis rolled over and looked at Clint. "Where's his home?"

"Maryland, I think."

"Has he ever given you any cause to think he isn't loyal?"

"No. Well . . . maybe no. I've heard him talk about States' Rights a few times. He was in Texas for some time. Some disloyal talk made an impression on him. At least that's my opinion."

"Someone is inciting the men to desert. I'm sure it's Carlie."

Clint whistled softly. "I'm penned up in that damned warehouse so much I've lost track of post gossip. What do you intend to do about it?"

"The major wants whoever is doing the talking to be brought up for court-martial."

"Now? With Cuchillo sitting out there watching us twenty-four hours a day?"

"Yes."

Clint stood up and filled two glasses with brandy. He handed one to Travis. "Be careful, Travis. It's a terrible thing to accuse an officer of."

Travis did not answer. Clint raised his head to look into Travis' eyes, then almost flinched at what he saw. "For God's sake, Travis," he

184

said quickly, "before you do anything rash you'd better make sure you're right."

Travis downed his drink and placed the glass on the table. "Where is he now?"

"Probably in his quarters. He's not on guard tonight."

Travis walked to the door.

"Do you want me to go with you, Travis?" asked Clint. "Ken has a hell of a temper. I've seen the killing rage in him. You might arouse it if you accuse him of treason."

Travis turned. "I can stand almost any kind of officer, Clint. God knows this post has one of the oddest assortments I've ever experienced. If I had the authority I'd cashier some of them right now. Some of them I like and some of them I dislike. I know for sure I hate one. Personally I like Ken Carlie, but if he's inciting treason on this post I'd just as soon kill him as look at him." Travis closed the door behind him.

Clint emptied his glass. He shook his head, remembering the cold look he had just seen in Travis Walker's eyes. Clint pulled on his shirt and then buckled his gun belt about his waist. When two men like Travis Walker and Kenneth Carlie got together with a bone of contention between them, someone was going to get hurt.

CHAPTER TEN

Travis rapped on the door to Carlie's quarters. The officer bunked alone in the last room of Officer's Row.

"Come in!" called Carlie.

Travis opened the door. Ken Carlie lay on his bunk, a book lying open on his chest. His left hand held a cigar, and in his right hand was his service pistol, cocked and pointed at Travis' belly. For one tense moment Travis thought the man suspected why he had come. A lump of ice seemed to form in his gut, and the instinct to go for his colt was hard to bridle.

Carlie smiled. He lowered the Colt, then let down the big hammer to half cock. "Good evening, Captain." He sat up and dropped his long legs over the side of the cot. "Sorry about your reception. I've spent too much time on outpost duty to take chances on accepting without question anyone who knocked on my door."

Travis nodded. He looked about the little room. It was hung with the usual pieces of clothing and equipment. A stout Indian bow hung on the rear wall over the washstand.

186

"Drink?" asked Carlie.

"No thanks. Just had one. I got back a little while ago from Santa Theresa."

"How was it?"

Travis dropped into a chair, out of line with Carlie's shooting hand. "Not bad. Things are beginning to get done."

"With Charlie Cass in charge? Times have changed."

"You don't have much of an opinion of him, Carlie."

"No . . . and neither do you."

Their eyes met. Under other circumstances Travis would have accepted the young officer as a kindred soul, for there was much in Carlie that matched Travis' thoughts and ways. "I'll take a cigar if you have one, Carlie," said Travis.

The box of cigars was on the little table at the foot of the cot. Carlie leaned toward it, reaching out with his right hand to get the box, moving himself out of position to get hold of his pistol in a hurry. As he did so, Travis stood up and walked toward the bed. He stopped just beside the Colt. "I think the major and myself have some questions to ask you, Carlie," he said quietly.

Carlie's hand stopped just over the cigar box. He turned his head to look up into Travis' eyes. Then he dropped his eyes to see Travis' hand resting on the butt of his revolving pistol. He knew right away he had been deliberately feinted out of position. "Concerning what, Captain Walker?" he asked.

"You'll find out when you get there, mister."

Carlie sat up straight. He knew better than to make a try for the pistol he wanted so badly. Travis would either draw and shoot or grapple with him, and Carlie wasn't so sure he could take the tall man in front of him.

"Get up and get ready," said Travis coldly.

Carlie stood up and reached for his shirt. He pulled it over his head, tied his scarf about his throat and reached for his gun belt, half expecting Travis to tell him to leave it hang, but Travis said nothing against his putting it on. He placed his hat on his head.

Travis picked up Carlie's Colt and let the hammer down easily. He passed it to Carlie butt foremost, and his eyes never left Carlie's. He wants me to try him, thought Carlie.

For a few seconds they stood there, and then Carlie raised the flap of his holster with his left hand and let the heavy six-shooter slip down inside the sheath. "I'd still like to know what this is all about," said Carlie.

"I think you do, mister."

How much did he know? Ken Carlie reached for the lamp to put it out.

"Leave it on, mister," said Travis. "Walk to the door."

Carlie walked to the door. The light went out behind him. Carlie had wanted to make a try for Travis in the darkness, but now he knew his broad back was silhouetted in the doorway. He walked out on the parade ground and waited for Travis.

Travis shut the door behind him. "Go on," he said. "You know where the major's quarters are."

Carlie turned his head and then smiled. "Senior officers first," he said.

Travis couldn't help but admire the man. "We'll walk together," he said.

Carlie turned to face Travis. "I know why you want me to go to the major. It's about the talking I've been doing."

"You don't have to talk to me, mister. It's up to Major Lester what to decide to do with you."

"You think he's got the guts to order me shot?"

"I have."

Carlie wet his lips. "Look," he said quickly, "you're in a hell of a spot here, Walker. You're the real commander of this fort. You'd be a hell of a lot better off if the old man wasn't here at all. Use your head."

"Keep talking. I'll give you another minute."

Carlie lowered his voice. "The morale here is bad enough as it is. Supposing you do accuse me of seditious talk and possibly of treason? Most of the men like me. Some of the officers do, too. If you bring me up to trail and have me shot, the morale will plummet to the bottom and you might lower it enough to hurt the defense of the fort if it is attacked."

"You sound like a damned guardhouse lawyer. Get moving."

"I haven't yet made my point."

"Go on, then."

"I've been planning for some time to resign and join the Confederacy. Let me leave here tonight, Walker, with my written resignation in your hands. You'll get no more trouble from me."

"It's a good thought, Carlie, except for one thing."

"So?"

"How far do you think you'd get from Fort Joslyn?"

Carlie rubbed a hand over his lean face. "By God, you'll not have me shot, Walker!"

"Get moving."

Carlie came a little closer to Travis. "What difference does it make to you?"

Travis raised a big hand and gripped the officer by the slack of his shirtfront. He drew Carlie closer. "You made the mistake of not resigning months ago, as other United States Army officers who sympathized with the South had the honor to do. No, you stayed around for a last stab in the back. Well, sonny, you stayed around a little too long!"

Travis shoved the officer back. For a moment Carlie stood there, then suddenly he sprinted for the corrals. Let him go, something seemed to say in the back of Travis' mind, but something else made him drop his hand to his colt. He ran forward. Carlie turned and drew. Travis jumped sideways as Carlie fired. Then the Colt seemed to leap into Travis' hand. The big hammer was thumbed back and the bullet sped into the power smoke that wreathed Carlie. Ken Carlie staggered forward. He tried to raise his smoking Colt, but the strength was draining from him. He dropped the heavy pistol and then reeled closer to Travis.

Men shouted in the background and boots thudded against the hard caliche. Ken Carlie raised his head and looked at Travis. "Damn you," he said. "I had a feeling you'd get me one way or another." He pitched forward on his face and lay still. A slow stain of blood spread across the hard earth beside him.

Travis stood under the ramada in front of his quarters, watching four enlisted men carryng off Ken Carlie's body. Clinton Vaughn stood beside Travis. "I had a feeling that was going to happen," he said quietly.

"That son of a bitch Walker killed Carlie without giving him a chance," a man said from near the civilian wagons.

"Ben Joad," said Clint.

"That's not true!" said Maggie Gillis.

A woman laughed. "You got a feeling under your dress for him, Maggie. Well, you won't get nowheres with his type. I oughta know."

There was the sound of flesh striking flesh. "Break it up, Maggie!" yelled Joad. "She's right. Besides, it ain't you nor any other civilian woman he's interested in. I think Carlie knew about him, and Travis Walker shut his mouth the only way he could. With a bullet in the belly!"

Clint Vaughn gripped Travis' arm. "Keep away from him," he said. "He's being doing some talking about you. Hinting at this and that."

Travis turned. "Such as?"

"Jesus! You don't want me to get involved, do you?"

Travis gripped the wrist of the hand which held his left arm. "Damn it! Talk? What does Joad mean?"

Clint winced as the steely fingers tightened. "All right," he said. "Come into the quarters."

Travis followed the quartermaster into the dark room. Clint lit the lamp. He walked back to the washstand and opened a drawer. He took something from it and handed it to Travis. Travis looked down at a filmy handkerchief. The faint aroma of jasmine rose to his nostrils. He looked up at Clint. "Well?" he asked.

Clint walked to the door and kicked it shut. "I found it on the floor the night you sent out those couriers. I don't know who left it here, Travis, but I can damn well guess."

Clint poured two drinks. "She's a lusty bitch," he said over his shoulder. "This is a lonely place. I can't say that I blame you."

Travis balled the handkerchief and threw it into the fireplace. "She was in here when I got here," he said. "The lamp was out. I damned near shot her."

"Maybe you should have. You shoot fast and well, Travis."

"Meaning?"

Clint shrugged. He turned and handed a glass to Travis. "Here," he said. "Drink this.

193

You'll need it when you talk to Enos Lester . . . God help you."

Travis downed the drink and felt it hit his belly like a dose of canister.

Clint leaned against the wall. "Someone must have seen her come in here or else leave. You know how gossip is on a post like this. Since then I've heard latrine rumors about something going on. It didn't surprise me about hearing her name. It *did* surprise me about hearing yours. God, but Charlie Cass can build this thing up into a dandy mess, and he's just the man to do it.

"There's nothing so outraged as a philandering husband or wife when they find out the tables have been turned."

"And what's your opinion, my philosophic friend?"

Clint waved his glass. "Look," he said quietly. "Until you showed up out here in the furthermost suburbs of hell I almost had *cafard*, as the French call the desert madness.

"Lester was slowly driving me mad. Cass made me sick. I could stand Carlie and Newkirk, but DeSantis irritated me to such an extent I nearly challenged him once. That might surprise you, looking at me, but I damned well meant to do it.

"Then there were other things. Evelyn Cass

switching her butt at every male on the post. Those civilians with their slatternly women. At first I thought they were just poor refugees. I should have known better."

"How so?"

Clint spat into the fireplace. "Have you seen any children among the lot of them? They represented themselves as honest frontier folk to old Enos, and he swallowed it hook, line and sinker. Some of them are as bad as the Apaches. At that, I'd almost trust Cuchillo more than I would Joad."

Travis nodded.

Clint straightened up. "So you see, Travis, you saved me from myself. I don't quite know how, but I'm grateful to you. Whatever you've done and whatever you do, I'm with you, and don't ever forget it."

"Thanks, Clint."

Clint reached into the fireplace and spread out the tight ball of handkerchief. He struck a block match and set fire to the filmy cloth. The two of them watched it burn.

Someone rapped at the door, and Travis opened it. A trooper saluted. "Captain Walker, sir, Major Lester wishes to see you in his quarters at once."

Travis returned the salute and nodded.

"Shall I go with you?" asked Clint.

"No sense in you listening to him on a hot

night like this. Besides, he'd probably order you to leave anyway."

Clint shrugged. "Marty Newkirk invited me over for a game. I'll be over there if you need me."

Major Lester was pacing back and forth in his heated room, swathed in a flannel robe. His loose slippers made a dry husking noise on the earthen floor. He whirled as Travis entered. "My God, Captain Walker!" he cried. "What have you done now?"

"The man was a traitor. The major himself said he'd court-martial and shoot any such man he found. I happened to find him. I was bringing him here. He made a break for freedom. I was almost willing to let him go, thinking the Apaches would deal with him soon enough. Mr. Carlie turned and fired at me. I killed him."

"Just like that?"

Travis nodded. "Just like that."

Lester mopped his dripping face. "How can I report this thing? I'll be brought up for investigation with you. It is only your word against perhaps a dozen others that Kenneth Carlie was a traitor."

"I'll take my chances on a court of investigation. Yes, and at a court-martial, too."

Lester's eyes seemed to bulge out. "Yes
196

. . . *you* will! But what about me? Within months of a promotion. Within a few years of a pension and honorable retirement. Did you think of my gray hairs and my forty years of service when you shot that man down?"

"No, sir."

"Well then, sir, just what *were* you thinking of?"

Travis couldn't help letting the ghost of a smile travel across his face. "Of a bullet in my belly, Major."

For a fraction of a second a change seemed to come over Enos Lester, as though he *had* been a real field soldier in years gone past and some of the power of command over a subordinate had mysteriously returned, but then the pudgy face sagged into the usual petulant expression of a man beset on all sides by tribulations over which he had no control.

"I'm sorry, Major," said Travis. "My sense of humor sometimes gets the best of me."

Lester dropped into his chair and rested his right elbow on the arm of the chair, cupping his sweating forehead in his hand. "A man comes in here with blood upon his soul. He puts his commanding officer in a terrible position. He jokes about killing a man. Just what and who are you, Mr. Walker?"

Travis did not answer. He felt no need for speaking, for Enos Lester did not expect

197

an answer. It was like trying to make intelligent conversation with a petulant child or a semisenile old woman.

Lester looked up. "You may leave, sir. I will not sleep a wink this night while trying to figure a way out of this latest dilemma."

"Good night, sir."

Travis softly closed the door behind him, then gratefully breathed in the fresh night air. Somewhere out in the night a coyote howled. Travis walked slowly toward his quarters. In the excitement of the night he had almost forgotten the principal peril to all the lives of Fort Joslyn and Santa Theresa – the Apaches – but *they* had not forgotten. With spidery patience they were weaving their almost invisible net about their quarry.

Travis paused for a moment, removing his hat to let the breeze dry the sweat on his forehead. A curtain was pulled aside in one of the windows of Captain Cass' quarters, and Evelyn Cass looked out at Travis with brooding eyes.

Travis walked on. Theresa crept easily into his thoughts and settled down in a corner of his mind like a contented kitten. She drove out the Apaches, Ken Carlie, Enos Lester and everything else.

Travis reached his quarters. Fort Joslyn and its intrigues sickened him as though it had a graveyard smell. He'd soft-talk the major into letting him return to Santa Theresa the next day. Somehow he seemed to know his future lay in the town rather than in the fort.

CHAPTER ELEVEN

The steady drumming of hoofs sounded like the rhythmic shaking of pebbles in a gourd rattle. Yellow dust swept ahead of the lone rider and shrouded him from the view of the men standing alertly at the gate of Fort Joslyn with cocked musketoons.

" 'Tis a Mex!" said Trooper Doherty. "I can see his hat!"

Travis Walker nodded. "Stand easy," he said.

The early afternoon sun beat down upon the fort, and there wasn't a breath of air on the desert. The hills were seen dimly behind a plum-colored haze. The horseman stood up in his stirrups and waved his hat at Travis. It was Jorge Valadez, the man who had helped Travis find the bodies of Maria Diaz and Teodoro Vaca. *"Hola, capitán!"* he yelled in a dust-hoarse voice.

"Hola, Jorge! Come on, man!"

199

Jorge drew in his big dun. He slid from the saddle and wiped the sweat from his broad face. "How goes it with you, Captain?"

"Forget the formalities. Why are you here?"

Jorge spat dryly. "There is touble in Santa Theresa."

"So?"

"Cuchillo struck at dawn, driving off many of our horses and mules. A house was burned down. A child was wounded, and two men and a woman died in the fight near the corrals."

"And the soldiers?"

Jorge looked up with hate in his eyes. *Them?* I urinate on them!"

Travis gripped the Mexican by his arm. "What the hell do you mean by that?"

Jorge raised his head. "They run wild in the town when you are not there. Captain Cass – I spit upon his name – does nothing to stop them from lolling in the *cantinas* and chasing the women of Santa Theresa. Our *alcalde* is much upset. He has sent me to see if you will come to Santa Theresa and take charge."

Travis nodded. "I'll talk to the major. Get some water. Tell Sergeant Ellis to have my horses saddled."

"*Sí, mi capitán.*"

Travis hurried to the major's office. The

commanding officer was working on a pile of papers. "Yes, Walker?" he asked.

"I'd like the major's permission to go into Santa Theresa on an inspection."

"Again?"

"I'd like to have the work well done, sir."

Lester rubbed his sweaty jaw. "Well, all right. One thing, however – take Mrs. Cass with you."

Travis jerked as though stung with a lash. *"Sir?"*

Lester did not look up. "Mrs. Cass is anxious to see her husband, poor lonely woman. I told her I'd let her go with you on your next tour of inspection."

"I haven't time to wait for her, sir."

Lester looked up. "So? Why?"

Travis bridled. He didn't want the nervous old man to know what had happened. "I'm sorry, sir," said Travis quietly. "I'll wait for her."

"Good! Be careful, Captain. I'll expect you back no later than tomorrow at noon, sir."

Travis nodded and saluted. He stamped out of the office. Evelyn Cass was standing under the ramada of her quarters, wearing a fashionable riding habit. She pulled on her gloves as Travis approached. "I'm ready," she said.

Travis eyed her closely. "How did you

201

know I was going into Santa Theresa?"

"Why, Captain! I knew your duty would force you to go back as quickly as possible. When I saw that Mexican courier I dressed as quickly as possible so as not to slow you down."

Travis looked into her, but there was no hint of guile in her immense eyes. "I'll see that you get a mount," he said.

"Don't bother. Kelligan is getting my mare."

Trooper Kelligan, as though he had received some sort of mental message from Evelyn Cass, was trotting her mare toward them.

Evelyn adjusted a scarf over her hat and across her face. "Poor Charlie misses me," she said.

Travis nodded. "I'm sure he does. Can hardly bear to be away from you." He walked toward his quarters. Jorge had Travis' horse ready.

"The woman goes along?" asked Jorge.

"Yes."

"This is madness!"

"It's the major's order."

"Then he is mad!"

Travis shrugged. He went into his quarters, took a stiff hooker, then got his weapons and gear. He walked outside. "Get Baconora,

Jorge," he said. "We might need him."

"*Sí!*"

Travis led his horse and Jorge's back to Evelyn. She had mounted her mare and sat sidesaddle, with the long skirt of her riding habit carefully draped over her long shapely legs. She smiled archly at Travis. "I knew I'd have my way," she said.

"I hope you're satisfied."

"I had to be with you one way or another."

"You will be until we get into Santa Theresa."

She adjusted her riding habit. "Oh, I don't know. Charlie won't bother much about me. I have a good idea about what he's doing there. I'll enjoy seeing you and Charlie have a nice friendly talk as officers and gentlemen."

She laughed at him. "I have a feeling I've dumped over your pretty little apple cart, Travis." She laughed again. "What's the great attraction in Santa Theresa?"

Travis did not answer. He saw Jorge and Baconora coming toward them. Then Travis turned. "I hope to God you can ride that mare, as well as being able to sit her there posing like a picture from Godey's Ladies Book."

She looked closely at him. "Why, Travis?"

He swung up onto his sorrel. "Because, Mrs. Cass, if we're jumped by Mimbrenos between here and Santa Theresa, you might have the ride of your life. To win that ride is to win your life; to lose it is to die."

She paled. For a moment she glanced uncertainly back at her quarters, then out toward the silent and sun-beaten desert. "You're trying to frighten me!" she said.

Travis shrugged. "Have it your way, Evvie." He grinned crookedly. "I'll save the last shot for you."

She bit her lip. Maybe she hadn't been so clever after all. "Perhaps you had better get an escort?" she suggested.

"From *here?* No, ma'am! There's hardly enough men here to stand guard. We go as we are and we go fast, and the devil – or Cuchillo Rojo, as the case may be – will take the hindmost."

Sergeant Mack Ellis stood under the ramada in front of headquarters and eyed Evelyn Cass. By God, she was a real filly, but absolutely forbidden for an enlisted man. Mack Ellis knew he was as good a man as any officer on the post, with the exception of Travis Walker. He knew damned well he was better than Charlie Cass, but not good enough to have a woman like Evelyn Cass to bed. Now she was riding into Santa Theresa along a desert road, under the greedy eyes of the watching Mimbrenos, and she was a sight good enough to make a man's head swim. It was too much for Mack Ellis. He wanted to be with her that long, anyway.

Mack Ellis walked forward and saluted Travis. "The captain is going into Santa Theresa?"

"Yes, Ellis."

"I'd like to go along, sir."

Travis eyed the big noncom. He wasn't the only one. Evelyn Cass never missed a chance to study any man who looked as though he had more than his share of masculinity.

"Well, sir?" asked Ellis.

"All right. Get moving."

Baconora swung up on his horse and hooked a leg about the big Mexican pie-plate pommel. "Quite a party this is getting to be," he said. "I'm looking forward to going into Santa Theresa. I here Ben Joad pulled out before dawn and went there." The scout eyed Evelyn. "Old Ben sure has a big mouth."

"What do you mean?" asked Travis.

"Nothing, Captain . . . nothing at all."

Ellis appeared, booted and spurred, leading his horse. The little cavalcade rode out past the guardhouse.

"Damned fools," said a trooper on guard to a lounging civilian.

"Oh, I don't know. With the exception of that Cass woman, I think that little party can damned well take care of itself."

The trooper grinned. "I know where she can beat all of them when it comes to taking care of herself."

The civilian spat. "That's for sure, Milligan. I'd like to try her myself."

There was no sign of Apaches as the five rode the dusty road toward Santa Theresa, raising a plume of saffron dust behind them. Not even a hawk sailed through the skies.

Halfway through the place where the low ridges crowded the rutted road, Evelyn Cass laughed. The four men turned to look at her, with varying emotions on their faces. "What is it, *señora?*" ask Jorge.

She pulled her filmy scarf from her face. "The four of you have been riding like boys past a graveyard at midnight, whistling to keep up your courage."

"So, *señora?*"

She thrust a gloved hand toward the deserted ridges. "What are you afraid of? There isn't even a jack rabbit on those ridges."

"Before God, *señora*, do not say such things! They may be watching us even now."

"Who, Jorge?"

"*Los Indios*. The Apaches."

She burst into laughter again. Mack Ellis

smiled. He loved to hear her full-throated laughter.

Baconora spat juicily. The amber hit the dust with the sound of a dropped pack of playing cards. "Yuh keep laughing like that," he said quietly, "and yuh might draw them outta those ridges."

"I'm not afraid."

"Yuh ever seen a bloodthirsty buck up close, Mrs. Cass? Yuh ever smell the grease on 'em? Yuh ever see what they do to white women?"

"Shut your gab!" said Ellis.

Baconora turned in his saddle. "I'm only trying to get some sense into her head."

"You're trying to frighten her."

Jorge looked at Travis and shrugged. Evelyn Cass studied Mack Ellis with new interest.

"Yuh saw that Maria Diaz out in the desert," said Baconora slowly. "Maybe this woman should have seen what was left of Maria."

Ellis drew rein and then leaned toward Baconora. "I told you to shut up, scout."

Baconora rested his hand on the butt of his Colt. "Yuh aimin' to make me, soldier?"

"Damn it!" Travis spurred his sorrel in between them. "While we're standing here like sitting ducks the Mimbrenos could

ambush us. Baconora! You ride ahead. Ellis!
You take the rear. Move! *Vámonos!*"

The two men did as they were bid, but a last
look of hate passed between them like clashing
blades.

Evelyn spurred her mare and rode ahead of
Travis and Jorge. Jorge crossed himself. "The
woman is a fool," he said.

Travis nodded. "In a way," he said dryly.

"The big *sargento* has his eyes on her all the
time."

"So? I hadn't noticed."

Jorge smiled. "The *capitán* has eyes for
many things. But some of the things right
beneath his nose he does not see. I do not
mean to offend, *capitán*."

Travis looked back at Sergeant Ellis. The
man dared not look at an officer's wife with
interest. Then Travis recalled how Ellis had
looked at her as he volunteered to accompany
the party into Santa Theresa. His defense
of her against Baconora seemed to be more
proof that the veteran had more than a
passing interest in Evelyn Cass. One woman
could raise more hell among woman-starved
troopers of an outpost garrison than the whole
Mimbreno tribe on the warpath.

Baconora was fifty yards ahead of them
now. Suddenly he turned his horse into tight
little circles, pointing with the carbine in his

hands toward the sand ridge to the west. It was the Indian sign for enemy in sight.

Travis looked toward the ridge. There Apaches sat their horses in full view, looking down at the little party below them. They did not move, and their weapons were not raised. Ellis closed up at a canter. "Sir!" he called out. "Look!"

Travis turned. Three more Apaches sat their mounts in the road behind them, just inside the mouth of the shallow pass.

"*Madre de Dios*," breathed Jorge. "Look! To the east!"

Three Apaches had appeared on the ridge-top as though they were ghostly puppets manipulated by unseen hands.

Travis looked to the north. The road was open.

"What shall we do?" asked Evelyn. There was a shaky huskiness in her voice.

Travis moved his horse to her right side. "We'll go on as we are," he said. "Jorge, stay on the left side of the *señora*. Let's move out."

Baconora waited a little until he was fifty feet ahead of the others, then rode steadily on toward Santa Theresa. Travis glanced sideways at Evelyn. There was panic riding her shapely shoulders, and panic could easily shift its load to the others. One scream would trigger the action and cause a stampede that would result in the deaths of all of them. But these men were veterans, used to the dangers of the open road in Apacheria, and they each knew that a wild break for freedom would have but one result.

"Do something!" pleaded Evelyn. She raised her head, and her neck muscles stood out sharply as the strain of her tension took control.

Travis looked away from her. Panic is an ugly sight, not to be looked upon by any man unless his control is exceptionally strong.

"Do something," she repeated.

The green smell of her fear seemed to overcome the feminine smell of her, usually carefully concealed by the artful use of jasmine. She was all woman now, stripped of any subterfuge, deathly afraid of those silent figures watching the small group on the dusty road.

Travis rode easily, reins in his left hand, right hand swinging freely by his side, looking straight ahead as though on parade. "Talk to me," he said out of the side of his mouth.

She shot him a look of intense fear. "Talk?"

"Yes, damn it."

"But those are Apaches, Travis."

"They won't attack us."

"How do you know? Do something, I tell you!"

Travis glanced at her. There was nothing attractive about Evelyn Cass now. "Talk," he said coldly. "If they had meant to attack they would have remained concealed until time to strike. They are guerrilla fighters, Evelyn. Their specialty is the quick raid and the ambush, never the hand-to-hand, last ditch fighting of the white man."

"Then why are they just sitting there watching us?"

"To put the fear of God into us."

Jorge looked ahead. "There is the town in the distance," he said.

"Let's make a run for it," said Evelyn. She raised her quirt but Travis leaned over toward her and gripped her wrist so hard she winced in pain.

"If we make a run for it, they'll lance in on us and cut us off one by one. So long as they are just sitting there we'll ride as though we were just out for a canter. Now talk pleasantly. Laugh. Above all – ignore them."

Baconora had dropped back toward them. He spoke over his shoulder. "There's Cuchillo Rojo," he said. "The one with the yellow-stained cow horns on his headdress riding that splotched apaloosa."

Travis slowly turned his head. The Mimbreno sat his gaudy horse on the highest

211

point of the western sand ridge. He was too far away from Travis to distinguish any of his features, but it wasn't really necessary, because an aura of hate and evil seemed to flow down the slope toward the party of white people. The cow horns thrust themselves out from a thick mat of some kind of fur, lending a grotesque and diabolical appearance to the war chief.

Jorge crossed himself and then thrust out his left hand toward the distant chieftain, first and little fingers extended, as though warding off the spell of a *brujo* wizard.

Ellis closed up behind Travis. "We can hold that crew off," he said.

"Yeah," said Baconora, "but they may have a whole damned war party hidden behind them hills."

The hoofs thudded steadily on the road, and the dust rose to wreath about the riders. The Mimbrenos did not move. Cuchillo Rojo still sat there, watching them as they rode past.

Suddenly Travis hated Cuchillo Rojo with all his soul. It was all part of the game he was playing with them. The eternal menace, with just enough harassment to keep the whites on a constant vigil, while the Mimbrenos came and went at will. Cuchillo Rojo, who could neither read nor write, was a master of psychological warfare and far more skilled at it than the educated professional soldiers he faced.

Travis could see the first buildings of the town, vague and ill-defined because of the shimmering heat waves which rose from the baking earth. Then they rode out into the clear. Suddenly a demoniacal cry tore through the quiet like the slushing of a saber. The bloodcurdling wail came again. Evelyn Cass swayed in her saddle. Travis gripped her and held her up. He looked back into the shallow pass. There was no sign of the Apaches in there now, nor on the low sand ridges. There was just a wraith of dust spiraling up in the faint wind.

Baconora spat. "That was Cuchillo," he said laconically.

"*Demonio!*" said Jorge.

Mack Ellis shoved back his hat and let the sweat sting his overheated face. "I'm glad that's over."

"It is – for a while," said Travis.

They rode on into the town, watched by silent townspeople. Travis drew rein in front of the *alcade's* house, then helped Evelyn to the ground. Her fingers dug into his arms as he did so, and he looked into her eyes. She was no longer the frightened woman of the pass but the wanton again, seeking Travis' attention.

213

Baconora had vanished, but his horse stood outside Jonas Simpson's *cantina*. Jorge slapped the dust from his clothing. "Baconora has the right idea," he said. "My legs are like water."

"Go with the sergeant and get a drink, then," said Travis.

Travis walked up onto the porch and hammered at the door until it was opened by Angelique. The woman smiled. "The brave *capitán!*" she said with a toothy smile.

"Good afternoon, Angelique. The Captain Cass is here?"

"No. He is in the town somewhere."

"This is his wife. Can she stay here until he returns?"

Angelique's expression did not change, but there was something in her eye as they surveyed Evelyn. It was as though she knew the seamy side of Captain Charles Cass and wondered what kind of woman would put up with him. "I am sure the *alcalde* will want her to stay. He is having his *siesta.*"

"And the *señorita?*"

Angelique smiled as though she shared a great secret with Travis. "She is in her room," she said. "I will tell her that the brave *capitán* is here."

"I'll take Mrs. Cass to her husband's room."

Angelique bobbed up and down, then vanished into a corridor. Travis took Evelyn down the long central corridor and out into the patio. Evelyn pulled the scarf from about her face and looked around the patio. "Beautiful," she said. "Charles always does well for himself. I hope the *alcalde* keeps a sharp eye on his young serving girls."

Travis looked away from her. There was a sour bitterness in her voice, and he wondered which of the two of them had failed the other. He guided her across the shady patio and opened the door of Charlie's room. She walked in and quickly raised her scarf across her nose. "Good God," she said thickly.

The low-ceilinged room stank of liquor slops, sweat-soaked clothing and the musty smell of a room which hasn't been aired in some time.

Evelyn Cass looked at Travis. "I almost expected to see half-gnawed beef bones on the floor among the rushes. Charlie would have made a fine medieval baron. You may be sure he doesn't leave our quarters at Fort Joslyn in *this* condition."

Travis nodded. He walked to the edge of the open patio. Theresa Morris had appeared at the far side. There was a catch in his throat, and his heart seemed to dash against his ribs. It was a feeling Travis had never experienced

215

before and he liked it, but mingled with it was a feeling of half melancholy.

Evelyn walked up to Travis. "The mistress of the house?"

"Señorita Theresa Morris, the *alcalde's* granddaughter."

Evelyn nodded. "I've heard of her. A rose blooming in the desert. I can see now why Charlie likes it here."

Travis turned a little." Be quiet," he said.

She studied him for a moment, glanced at the girl, then back at Travis. "So that's it," she said softly.

Theresa was almost upon them now. She held out a slim hand to Travis, and the touch of it was like a key to another world – a world of promise and love. *"Señorita Morris,"* said Travis, "this is the wife of Captain Cass, Evelyn Cass."

Theresa bowed her head a little. "It is a pleasure to meet you, *señora.*"

"Thank you, *señorita.* I have heard a great deal about you."

Their eyes met, and to Travis it seemed as though invisible blades had been thrust out, had made contact as though to test their opponent's mettle, then had been withdrawn for another, later trial.

"I am sorry the captain is not here, Mrs. Cass," said Theresa.

216

"It is quite all right. The captain probably has many duties which require his absolute attention." There was the faint mingling of scorn and bitterness in the older woman's voice.

"Yes," said Theresa quietly.

"I'll wait in his room," said Evelyn.

"You will stay the night?"

Evelyn shrugged. "I'll see."

Travis eyed her. "I'll not be leaving here much before late tomorrow morning, Evelyn."

"In that case I'll accept your invitation," said Evelyn to Theresa.

Theresa smiled. "I'll have Angelique straighten up the captain's room."

She shook her head. "No," she said, as though reluctant to have even a serving woman see the mare's nest in the room. "I'll do it myself."

"But . . ."

Evelyn raised her head. "It's quite all right," she said coolly. "I must have something to do until he gets back." She walked into the room and closed the door behind her.

Travis drew the girl close and kissed her. For a moment her lips blended with his, and then she drew back. "Someone might be looking," she said.

"I'm worried."

She laughed. "You sound like it. Anyway, we have all day and tonight to see each other."

"Not today, Theresa. I came into town to see about that raid."

"And not to see me?" she pouted.

He grinned. "I'll admit I was planning to think of an excuse to come in. But I'm here now, and we have this evening to be together."

She leaned back against a post. "Cuchillo has been seen in the hills. It is said he led the raid himself. I have never seen him, Travis. What is he like?"

"I saw him for the first time today. That is, I saw him at a distance. I don't really know what he looks like."

She looked up at him. "You have a great deal of respect for him, don't you?"

"In a way. He's diabolically clever."

"He has said that he will rule this country from the Peloncillos to the Rio Grande and from the Gilas far down into Chihuahua."

"We'll see about that."

"How can you stop him? He has many warriors and many fine guns. He knows the country. The soldiers are penned up at Fort Joslyn, and we people of Santa Theresa dare not travel the roads as we did for so many years. Who is there to stop him, Travis?"

"I don't know. Sometimes I feel as though we whites will never know this country as the Apaches do. Perhaps it was never meant for us to rule over it."

She placed a hand on his arm. "You're worried. I can feel it. What has been happening at the fort?"

"Nothing but routine."

Her dark eyes held his. "That is not true. Something has happened there which has scarred you deeply. I *know*, Travis. It seems as though you are never very far away from me. It seems as though I know everything of which you think."

He thrust out his right hand, first and little fingers extended. "*Bruja* witch," he said teasingly.

She shrank back a little, and her face paled. "Travis! Please don't joke about it."

He drew her close and kissed her. "I'm sorry. Come with me to the door."

They walked across the patio with their arms about each other's waists. The door of Charles Cass' room swung open, and Evelyn Cass stood there and watched them walk across the shade-dappled patio. Her mouth drew down tightly, and she gripped her throat with her right hand. Then she turned to look at the mess her husband had left behind. She spat into the fireplace.

Travis stood at the door and looked down at Theresa. "Tonight then?"

"Tonight," she promised.

He kissed her, then left the house. The sun was beating down on the dusty plaza. He turned and looked back at the house. He felt a raging impulse to go back for Theresa and take her away from there, at night, to strike for the Rio Grande. But he knew it was hopeless. It would end up with him penned down in some arroyo, shooting it out to the last, saving the last bullet for the woman he loved. No, there was nothing for him to do but stay on duty, hoping and praying for some guidance which would help him defeat Cuchillo Rojo. The prospect was pretty damned gloomy.

CHAPTER TWELVE

Travis walked across the plaza toward the town corrals. There was the usual coterie of gamblers playing monte under a sagging brush ramada. One of them looked up from beneath a huge steeple hat. "It's the *bravo*," he said. "Hey, Captain!"

Travis turned to look at the little man

called Vince. Vince grinned. "Looks like old Cuchillo ain't much afraid of you soljer boys here," he said loudly.

The gamblers laughed. Vince stood up and leaned against a post. "Some garrison we got," he jeered. "The commanding officer spends most of his time drinking and chasin' wimmen and the rest of the time sleepin' off a drunk."

Jorge crossed the plaza toward Travis. "Let me handle him," he said to Travis.

"Let him talk. He's just looking for trouble."

Vince spat. "You soljers oughta let *real* men take over here. Whyn't you scuttle off to the Rio Grande like the rest of the garrisons? Yuh ain't doin' a damned bit of good here."

"Hear him!" screamed a woman. "My husband was killed at the corrals and my baby son was wounded by those cursed Apaches while the soldiers played in the *cantinas!*"

"She is right," said a pock-faced man.

A crowd had begun to gather near Travis. They eyed him hotly. Jorge whispered to Travis. "I do not like the looks of this."

Hands rested on knives. Vince swaggered out from beneath the ramada. Then two men appeared from Simpson's *cantina* and walked toward Travis and Jorge. It was Mack Ellis and Baconora. They walked right through the center of the milling crowd, shoving the small

Mexicans aside. Ellis grounded his musketoon as he reached Travis' side, and Baconora hefted his rifle. The crowd drew back a little. It was a rugged quartet they faced.

Vince came forward. "Well, Captain," he sneered. "What have you to say for the United States Army?"

"Keep quiet," said Baconora. "You always did talk too much, Vince."

"Let me get at him, sir," pleaded Ellis.

Travis looked at the crowd. They were angry, and they probably had a right to be. Travis had not seen a soldier of the town garrison since he had arrived in Santa Theresa. More of the townspeople began to drift toward the threatening crowd.

"We oughta run all these damned soljer boys outta *our* town," said Vince.

Baconora laughed. "Listen to him," he jeered. "Been run out of every town in New Mexico and now he calls Santa Theresa *his* town."

"I wonder what his angle is," said Mack Ellis quietly to Travis.

"I don't know, Sergeant, but he's got these people eating out of his dirty hands."

Hoofs thudded on the hard caliche of the plaza, and a dusty horseman, followed by half a dozen others, appeared near the corrals. The leader was Captain Charles Cass. His face was reddened by the sun, and sweat streaked through the dust coating it.

"Where's he been?" called out Vince. "Chasing 'Pache squaws through the brush?"

Cass swung a thick leg over his saddle and dropped to the ground. He walked toward Travis with the stiff-legged walk of a weary man. He saluted casually. "I didn't expect to see you, Walker," he said.

"I learned there had been a raid here."

Cass nodded. "I pursued some of the Apaches."

Travis looked beyond the big officer. "With *six* men?"

Cass waved his arm. "It was all I needed to teach those filthy beggars a lesson."

"What lesson?" called out Vince.

Cass turned. "Armstrong!" he yelled. "On the double!"

A lanky trooper came forward carrying a heavy sack.

"Open it," said Cass.

Armstrong cut the draw string. Two rounded objects thudded to the ground like heavy melons.

"Jesus," said Ellis. "Apache heads."

"Yeh," said Baconora dryly. "And wimmen's heads to boot."

"Squaws!" said Jorge.

Travis looked down at the bloody, dusty

heads, dotted with buzzing flies. "Get them out of sight," he said thickly.

Armstrong casually picked them up by the hair and dropped them into the sack. The crowd was terribly quiet. Cass took off his Kossuth hat and slapped the dust from his clothing. "We caught them near the big dry wash three miles from here. Dropped them as neat as you please at no less than one hundred and fifty yards, offhand."

"Were there any warriors with them?" asked Travis.

"No. Why do you ask?"

"You would have never made it back here if there had been. What did you do with the bodies?"

Cass grinned. "Left them for the ants and the *zopilotes*, what else?"

Travis looked over the heads of the crowd toward the heat-hazy hills. "Cuchillo and his warriors will never rest until they find the man who killed those two squaws. God help him when they do."

Cass paled beneath the dust on his face. "They didn't see us close up, I'll warrant."

"They know you were soldiers. At least they know you were wearing uniforms."

"Just what do you mean by that, sir?"

Travis eyed the big officer. "You figure it out, Cass. *You figure it out . . .*"

The crowd had begun to break up, drifting toward the *cantinas* and the shade of their homes. Vince had returned to his game of monte, but Travis could feel the little man's eyes studying him as he walked toward the Morris house.

Travis spoke over his shoulder. "Sergeant Ellis, rout out every man jack of this garrison. Have them line up at the *torreon*. Baconora, you take a ride toward the hills to see what Cuchillo is up to. Jorge, warn the people that they must stay close to their homes and have their weapons ready at all times."

"I thought I was in command here," protested Cass.

"You are – under me, Cass."

"I punished those raiders, didn't I?"

"You're lucky you got back at all. Thank God Cuchillo and his warriors were watching us come into town. If he had found those women and cut you off in the desert, you would have died a hellish death, Cass."

"I'm not afraid of Apaches."

Travis turned as he reached the porch of the mayor's house. "I believe you, Cass. You're brave, but you're ten kinds of a damned fool."

"Take care how you talk!" blustered Cass.

Travis smiled thinly. "I haven't even begun to talk. I'd have you up for court-martial if we didn't need you."

225

"Well, thanks, damn you!"

Travis felt for a cigar and lit it. "You're damned lucky Cuchillo didn't decide to take the whole *placita* while he was running off those horses and mules."

"We were on duty."

"Where?" Travis eyed Cass through the smoke. "In the *cantinas* or the *casas de putas?*"

Cass raised a big freckled fist. "You go too far, Walker!"

Travis took the cigar from his mouth. "Go on into the house and cool off. Your wife is waiting for you."

The remark took Cass as though a six-pounder shot had hit him in the belly. "Evelyn? *Here?*"

Travis nodded. "I came in to see about that raid. Major Lester said she was to go along to see you."

Cass' pale eyes studied Travis. "Very touching," he said.

"It was her idea, Cass. I'm not so sure she thought it was a good idea when Cuchillo and some of his warriors sat their horses on the sand ridges and watched us go by."

There was no flicker of emotion in the big officer's eyes. It was almost as though he had said he had wished Cuchillo *had* gotten Evelyn.

Travis settled his hat on his head and took a
226

drag at his cigar. "See you," he said briefly.

Cass watched Travis walk toward the *torreon*. Then he closed his big fists and spat deliberately on the ground where Travis had just walked.

The long afternoon had dragged by with nothing to break the monotony. Travis had inspected the little garrison. Some of the men were obviously suffering from hangovers. Travis had decided to assign First Sergeant Mack Ellis to the garrison. Ellis would keep the men in line if anyone could, and it was a cinch that Charlie Cass was so absorbed in his own pleasures he'd probably welcome the big noncom to take some of the responsibilities from his shoulders.

Baconora came in at dusk and reported to Travis. "Ain't much doing around here, Captain," he said. "Tracks seem all to head to the southwest, probably to those hills west of Fort Joslyn. It's my guess that Cuchillo might be aimin' to give the post some trouble."

Travis nodded. "Hit Santa Theresa, then hit Fort Joslyn. I wanted the major to either garrison the town *or* the fort, but not both."

Baconora whittled a fresh chew. "I found them bodies in the desert. Dumped them into a gully and covered them with rocks and brush. I hope to God the coyotes don't

227

drag 'em out again. If Cuchillo saw what Cass had done, I wouldn't give a used chew of this tobacco for his chances of leaving New Mexico alive."

Baconora stuffed the chew into his mouth and worked it into pliability. He grinned. "Jesus, what a ball they'd have with that big bastard once they got at him with their knives and their little torture fires."

Travis looked out toward the dim hills. "Keep an eye open tonight, Baconora. Get some food and then keep on patrol. Maybe Jorge Valadez will spell you."

"You don't think Cuchillo will hit 'em here again, do you?"

"I don't know anything except that Santa Theresa is one big target for Cuchillo any time he feels like hitting it. There isn't too much he can do at Fort Joslyn, except make nuisance raids and cut off anyone who leaves the post. But here he can strike whenever he pleases, and the raid he just made was just a token of what he can do."

"Yeah. Where can I find you if I need you?"

"At the Morris *casa.*"

Baconora's reddish eyes studied Travis. "Yeah," he said quietly. "I figured as much." He walked silently off into the darkness.

Travis walked about the wide plaza. Sentries were on duty here and there.

A cool finger of breeze felt Travis' wet forehead as he stood near the corrals. A mule bawled noisily. Somewhere behind Travis in the *cantina* a guitarist softly strummed away. It seemed so peaceful, but the night was like a great sleeping tiger, soft of fur, with rounded pads on all four feet. But that tiger could easily awaken and bare fangs and sharp claws from the softness to rend and tear.

Travis walked toward the Morris *casa*. He had been invited to stay the night at the mayor's house and to have dinner there. He hadn't seen Charlie Cass all afternoon, nor had he seen Evelyn. He wondered how those two lovable people, man and wife, had been getting along. He grinned to himself.

Travis looked toward the old *torreon*. He could see a steeple-hatted Mexican on guard atop the structure. Two men stood outside Jonas Simpson's *cantina*. One of them was Charles Cass, but it took a moment for Travis to recognize the other one until the man lit a lucifer to ignite his pipe. It was then he recognized the saturnine face of Ben Joad, badly marked by the healing scar of the burns he had suffered when Travis had knocked him into the fire at Fort Joslyn.

Travis stepped behind a building buttress and watched the two men. Joad was talking swiftly, and as he did so Cass nodded again

229

and again. Then Cass clapped Joad on the back and walked toward the Morris *casa*. Joad lounged into the *cantina*.

Travis rubbed his jaw. It seemed that everywhere he looked he saw enemies. He cursed himself for stopping at Fort Joslyn and then realized his foolishness. If the fort had not been there he might have been killed by the Mimbrenos and even now be drying out in the desert. Then, too, he might not have met Theresa, and she alone was worth all the trouble he was exposed to. Again he had the impulse to get her and take her away from Santa Theresa, but he knew the futility of it. Sink or swim, live or die, their lives were immutably bound with the course of events that would take place at Santa Theresa.

The candlelight glistened softly on the polished furniture in the dining room of the Morris *casa*. It also glistened as softly, but with infinitely more warmth on the bared shoulders of Theresa Morris and Evelyn Cass. Charlie Cass was feeling his liquor again, but his eyes were constantly on Theresa rather than on his wife. It was a good thing that James Morris could not see what was going on at his table.

Travis leaned back in his chair. Now and then the level gaze of Evelyn Cass' great eyes met his. She had been drinking wine steadily all through the course of the meal, and her clear skin was flushed and delicately dewed with sweat. In contrast, Theresa looked as cool as the night wind sweeping across the desert. She studiously avoided Charles' gaze, but Travis knew she disliked his scrutiny of her. Charlie Cass had a way of undressing a woman with his eyes, and most women could feel the sensation.

James Morris sipped at his wine. "It is a pleasure to have two such gallant soldiers at my table," he said. "Santa Theresa is fortunate indeed to have such defenders."

"Thank you," said Travis.

Charlie Cass emptied his wineglass and quickly refilled it. "Don't worry about Santa Theresa or *Theresa* for that matter, while I'm here, Morris."

Evelyn slowly turned her head to look at Theresa, then at her husband, then at Theresa again. "I'm sure Charles would defend *any* woman to the death," she said.

Charlie turned to look at her, and there was pure hate in his pale eyes. "Including *you*, my dear?"

Evelyn Cass looked away from him. "I should hope so, Charles dear."

Angelique bustled in to clear the table. Travis leaned toward Theresa. "It is quite warm in here. Would you like to walk in the patio?"

She smiled. "If it is all right with Grandfather."

The old man seemed lost in a world of his own. "Yes," he said. "I am retiring soon. It has been a long day."

Travis stood up and drew back Theresa's chair, damnably conscious of Evelyn's hot eyes on him. Charlie Cass was refilling his wineglass. Nice place you have here, Morris. Quite an inheritance for someone." He looked at Theresa.

Theresa flushed. She adjusted her mantilla over her comb and hair. James Morris brushed back his white hair. "Yes. It all goes to Theresa. The house and money. Mining properties here and in Mexico. Then, too, there is the large house in Santa Fe, which I own as well as other properties there and in Albuquerque. She will want for nothing when I am gone."

"A fine dowry for the lucky man," said Cass.

Morris seemed a little annoyed. "Help me to my room, Angelique," he said. "You must excuse me, my guests."

Angelique helped the old man from the room. Evelyn Cass looked at Theresa. "You're very fortunate," she said. "Some lucky man will live comfortably for the rest of his days with you." Her eyes seemed to drift toward Travis.

Charles hiccupped . "Yes," he said thickly. "And Travis Walker might make it yet."

Travis turned but he felt the gentle pressure of Theresa's hand on his arm. "Please," she whispered.

Travis guided her to the door and into the hall. He shut the door behind him, hearing Cass' loud laughter. Theresa looked up at Travis. "That man frightens me," she said.

"Don't worry about him. I taught him one lesson."

"Do you think it was a permanent one?"

Travis opened the door at the end of the hall and felt the cool night breeze blow in from the patio. "I can always do it again."

"You're worried, aren't you?"

"A little."

"Don't avoid the question, Travis. Tell me."

He closed the door behind him and took her by the arm. "Yes, I am. I don't like conditions at the fort, and I like them a lot less here in Santa Theresa. I'd like to get you out of here, Theresa, but it is impossible until we meet and defeat Cuchillo."

"If you *do* defeat him. What if you don't?"

He closed her soft mouth with a kiss. "You

know what will happen. One way or another we must defeat him."

She looked up at the stars. "I would not leave here anyway," she said quietly. "I will not leave my grandfather nor the people I have known most of my life."

They paced to the west end of the patio. A night bird chirped from the clinging vines. It seemed so quiet and peaceful there.

"Why did she come here?" asked Theresa.

"Mrs. Cass? Why, to see her husband."

The girl looked up at Travis. "I don't think so. There is no love between those two. They are bound together by a marriage which certainly was never formed in the eyes of God."

He passed a hand across her smooth cheek. "Little wise one," he said softly. "Let's talk about us."

"What is she to you, Travis?"

"Nothing."

"The way she *looks* at you!"

"She looks that way at many men."

"She does not look at her husband like that."

Travis shrugged. "I'm sorry for the two of them."

There was a faint silvery touch of moonlight in the eastern sky. The night wind whispered through the vines and the leaves of the shade

234

trees. Travis drew her close and kissed her. A door opened, and yellow lamplight flooded into the patio, revealing Travis and Theresa to Evelyn Cass. Evelyn walked toward the room she shared with her husband. She turned to look squarely at them. "Good night," she said. The door closed behind her.

"It's getting late," said Travis. "Look – there is Angelique."

The serving woman had opened the hall door and stood there, looking at them. "It is late, *señorita!*" she called.

"My *duenna*," said Theresa. She laughed softly. "As though I weren't safe with you, Travis."

"Don't be so sure. I only have so much resistance."

She touched his face. "There will be a day when I will not expect to meet such resistance." She walked swiftly toward her room on the north side of the patio.

"Wait!" called Travis.

She shook her head. She nodded to Angelique, and the serving woman followed Theresa into her room. The door clicked shut behind them.

Travis lit a cigar and walked toward the main body of the house. He could see yellow lamplight in Cass' room. Evelyn had brought a gown with her, and she had worn it for one

235

purpose – to excite Travis that night. But she had not reckoned on Theresa. Travis was almost willing to admit he was glad that Theresa had been between him and Evelyn, for the older woman was certainly more than just attractive.

Travis opened the hall door and paced down the cool hall. The dining-room door was ajar, and he heard the smash of glass. He looked in. Charlie Cass lay with his arms and head on the white tablecloth amid a litter of broken wineglasses and scattered bits of food. The wine had stained the cloth blood red, as though Cass had bled his life away as he lay there.

Travis shook his head in disgust. He shut the door and walked to the greater outer door of the *casa*. He took his hat from a hook and walked outside. The moon was silvering the western slopes of the mountains to the east. It was as quiet as the grave – a rather gruesome simile, thought Travis, as he walked about the plaza.

The sentries were still on duty. Here and there a seraped Mexican stood at his post. There were few lights on in the town other than those of the *cantinas*, which never seemed to shut their doors.

Sergeant Ellis appeared out of the dimness

like a great genie. "Good evening, sir," he said.

"How does it go, Sergeant?"

"Quiet, sir – too damned quiet, begging your pardon, Captain."

"Where's Baconora?"

"Prowling about somewhere. He gives me the creeps the way he moves about. One minute you see him, the next minute he's gone. I'll swear to God, sir, that man moves quieter than an Apache."

Travis leaned back against the warm wall behind him. "You don't have much use for him, do you, Ellis?"

"I didn't say that, sir!"

"You didn't have to."

The big noncom studied Travis. "I didn't like the way he spoke to Mrs. Cass is all, sir."

"He spoke the truth."

"The lady was frightened enough as it was."

"I won't argue about that."

"Will she stay here, sir? That is, I mean, she won't go back to the fort with you tomorrow?"

Travis relit his cigar. "I hope not," he said.

"It's dangerous enough for men out there, sir."

Travis puffed his cigar into life. "Yes," he said quietly. Evelyn Cass could make it damned dangerous for any man in Fort Joslyn or Santa Theresa. He remembered what Clint

237

Vaughn had said about her: *Evelyn Cass is quite a woman. In fact she's all woman, with most of the faults and few of the virtues, but she can still turn the eye of every man on this post except two.* One of those men had been her husband, and the other Major Lester.

Travis looked at the first sergeant. The man was carrying a bitch of a crush on Evelyn Cass. Maybe Mack Ellis was the type of man she should have married, instead of her drinking, skirt-chasing husband.

"Well good night, Sergeant," said Travis.

"Good night, sir."

Travis walked back to the Morris *casa*. He rapped on the door until old Esteban opened it. Travis walked to the dining room. Charlie Cass still lay there, his face pasted to the cloth by liquor slops. The candles guttered and flared in the draft from the open door. A vigil light also shone before the carved wooden *santo* in the wall-niche. The impassive Indian-looking face of the crude carving seemed to be studying the drunken man who lay across the table.

Travis shook his head and walked to the patio. There were no lights. He walked across to the room which had been alloted to him on the west side of the patio. He walked into it and lit a candle. It was a big room, and clean as a barracks just before Saturday inspection.

The tiled floor had been waxed and polished, and the walls had been freshly whitewashed, while coarse *gerga* cloth had been hung along the lower parts of the walls to protect the clothing against contact with the whitewash.

Travis stripped to his drawers and washed himself. He combed back his thick hair and walked to the window which opened to the west. He unlatched the thick shutters and let them swing open so he could see the distant moon-washed hills. There was no sign of life on the desert west of the town.

Travis was about to get into bed when he thought of something. Cuchillo might raid again, and the next time he raided he might go full out. Travis pulled on his trousers, placed his boots close by the side of the bed and put his gun belt and holstered Colt on the chair beside the bed. He blew out the candle and lay down on the bed, lacing his fingers behind his neck, staring at the ceiling, thinking of Theresa.

CHAPTER THIRTEEN

Maybe it was the cool breeze flowing through the open window that awakened Travis; maybe it was the distant wailing of a coyote; maybe it was a subtle warning deep in the subconscious. He opened his eyes and looked up at the dim ceiling. He shivered a little in the cold and reached for the thick blanket which was folded at the foot of the big bed. Then he raised his head. There was nothing but the usual night sounds, but he still felt as though something were warning him.

He swung his legs over the side of the bed, wincing as his bare feet struck the cold tiles. He pulled on his socks and boots and took his Colt from its holster. He padded to the window and looked out upon the desert. The moon was gone, but there seemed to be an unnatural and eerie light on the waste lands. Travis pulled the shutters to and placed the bar across the rests.

He walked to the door and opened it, stepping out onto the patio. The breeze rustled the shade trees and vines, and he could hear the wash of water against the sides of the fountain bowl. The odors of flowers were mingled with those of sage and mesquite from the desert, wafted across the walls by the ceaseless wind.

There were no lights visible. Travis shrugged and turned to go back to bed, but something again arrested him. He walked softly toward the south side of the patio where the Cass room was. There was no light or sound from it, and the door was closed. He walked to the eastern side of the patio. All the doors were closed.

Travis rubbed his jaw. He felt like a damned fool, prowling about in the dimness. He walked up the northern side of the patio. Then he saw that Theresa's door was ajar. He was about to pass toward his own room when he heard what he thought was harsh breathing and, a moment later, the ripping of cloth. Travis pushed the door open. "Theresa!" he called out.

There was a muffled sound, and then a grunt. "Theresa!" he called again. He pushed the door wide open. Then, intermingled with the perfumed feminine odor of the room, he caught an odor he recognized at once – the sour, clinging and acrid sweat odor of a man. He knew damned well who it was – Charles Cass. There was a muffled curse from the darkness, and then Theresa screamed.

Travis lit a match, and, in the flickering

241

light, he saw the girl standing in a corner of the room, holding the shreds of her nightdress about her body. Her eyes were wide, and her dark unbound hair hung across her face.

Charles Cass stood in the center of the room, staring at Travis. He was dressed only in his trousers. His broad face was dewed with sweat, mingled with trickling blood from a number of deep scratches. His eyes were glazed, and his mouth hung open, a trickle of spittle coming from it. The match seared Travis' fingers at the same time Charlie Cass charged.

Cass butted into Travis with all his weight, driving him back against the door, which smashed shut behind him. The Colt flew from Travis' hand as his head hit the door. Cass stood there, legs wide apart, hammering home vicious blows that held Travis against the door. He planted both hands on the sweaty, bloody face of the big officer, pushing up on his palms, clawing at Cass' nose and eyes with his fingertips. Cass gasped and fell back in time to receive a left to the mouth that drove him back against the end of the big wooden bed.

Cass cursed as he charged again. Travis moved back, covering his belly against the triphammer blows of the heavier man. He fell over a stool and staggered sideways, just as Cass threw a sledgehammer right which skinned past Travis' head and glanced from the wall. Cass emitted a hoarse animal-like scream. Travis swung his left arm in a backhander, the edge of his hand striking hard at the base of Cass' neck, driving the big man against the wall.

Cass slid to the floor and instantly grappled for Travis' legs, dumping him sideways. The sweat-stinking officer rolled atop Travis and clawed at his face. His breath was sour with liquor, and he fought in a frantic way, utilizing every dirty trick he knew, but he was beginning to tire. The alcohol which had sparked him was now turning against him.

Travis brought a knee up into Cass's groin. The man grunted in pain. He raised himself, and Travis drove in short, chopping blows to his face until he rolled free from Travis and into a patch of dim light on the floor. He saw the Colt close at hand and grabbed for it, but Travis was too fast. He planted a boot heel on Cass' wrist and ground down as hard as he could. The big man cursed.

Travis stepped back and, as Cass sat up, drove a boot heel home to his jaw, smashing him back against the foot of the bed. Cass lay still. Travis reached for the Colt.

"No, Travis!" screamed Theresa.

The killing urge suddenly left him. He

thrust the Colt beneath the waistband of his trousers, then handed Theresa a blanket from the bed. She wrapped herself in it. Travis lit a lamp. He picked up a pitcher from the washstand and dumped the contents over the battered mess of a man on the floor. Cass gasped and spluttered. He got to his feet and raised his big fists.

"Cass," said Travis thinly. "I should have killed you. If you make one move I *will* kill you."

Theresa moved close to Travis. "I was asleep. I felt his hands on me and awoke to look up into his face. He is mad with liquor."

"It's more than that," said Travis.

Cass wiped the blood from his face. "Who are you to talk?" he asked thickly.

"What do you mean?"

Cass laughed. He looked at Theresa. "The whole damned post knows about him. Travis Walker, the *bravo!* Yeah, the lover!"

"I don't understand," said Theresa quietly.

The reddened eyes turned to look at Travis. "Took advantage of me being gone on duty to dally with my wife. Don't deny it, Walker! She was seen leaving your quarters. Ben Joad's woman told him, and he told me."

Cass walked unsteadily to the door. He turned. "If you don't think there is something going on between him and my wife, Theresa, maybe you can remember how she kept looking at him during dinner tonight." He closed the door behind him.

Theresa walked away from Travis. "Well?"

"The woman came into my quarters, Theresa."

"Then you don't deny it?"

"She came to my quarters and I sent her away."

Theresa turned away and rested a hand against the wall. "Thank you for saving me from him."

"Is that all you have to say?"

She turned to face him. "Yes. Please leave."

He walked toward her and held out his arms. She turned away again. "Please let me alone," she said.

"Let me explain."

"It isn't necessary."

Travis picked up his Colt. "Good night, then," he said.

She nodded.

Travis walked outside and shut the door behind him.

Theresa Morris threw herself on the bed, and sobs racked her body as she beat on the covers with her small fists . . .

Charles Cass knelt by the fountain, splashing water over his face and upper body. Travis stopped behind him. "Get out of here the first thing in the morning," he said. "If I so much as see you around this house I'll kill you."

Travis walked to his room and closed the door behind him. He took a cigar and lit it, dropping into a big armchair. There was hell to pay now. He felt sick inside. He closed his eyes and rested his head back against the chair. Damn Charlie Cass and his wife. They had been nothing but trouble for him ever since he had arrived at Fort Joslyn.

A cold early morning wind swept across Santa Theresa. Travis left his room with his gear and walked across the patio, hoping to get out of the house without seeing anyone, but he was doomed to disappointment. The door of the Cass room swung open and Evelyn Cass appeared, wearing her riding habit. "Travis!" she called out.

He stopped and turned to face her. She came up to him. "Are we going back today?"

"Evelyn, I don't give a damn what you do."

She studied him. "I think I know what happened last night. Charlie got a terrible beating. He left at dawn."

"Where did he go?"

"I don't know, and I don't really care."

"Nice," said Travis dryly.

"Take me back with you."

246

"You've got me in enough trouble now."

"What do you mean?"

He eyed her coldly. "You know damned well what I mean."

"Charlie said something about it when he came in last night. He says he won't have anything more to do with me."

"What can you expect?"

She flushed. "Do you think it has been easy living with that animal?"

"You haven't done so badly yourself, Evelyn."

She stepped back. "Damn you! I'm glad I came to your quarters. I'm glad I started a scandal about you. Most of all, I'm glad I've wrecked your chances with that young bitch."

Travis' right hand caught her full across the cheek. She staggered back with the blow, and quickly raised her hand to the reddening flesh. There were tears in her big eyes. Travis walked away from her and did not look back.

Jorge Valadez met Travis near the *torreon*. "There is a message from Cuchillo," he said quietly.

"So?"

Jorge turned and whistled. A peon, dressed in ragged and dirty white, shuffled forward taking off his battered hat. "This is Timoteo Castro," said Jorge. "A muleteer. He does not speak the *Ingles*."

"What does he have to say?"

"He says he was in the sand hills trying to find one of his mules when he was surrounded by Apaches. Cuchillo Rojo prevented them from killing him. Cuchillo, who speaks Spanish well, told Timoteo the message he wanted taken to *Alcalde Morris*."

"Keep talking."

Timoteo began to speak in a trembling voice. "Cuchillo says he is not afraid of the soldiers. That he is the greatest of war chiefs. That men tremble when he rides the earth."

"Go on!" snapped Travis.

Timoteo swallowed. "He says there are certain conditions which must be met if he is to leave Santa Theresa alone. He wants twenty horses and ten mules. He wants arms and ammunition, food and blankets." The little muleteer's voice trailed off.

"Go on," prompted Jorge.

The big brown eyes lifted to look at Travis. "There is one other thing, *mi capitán*."

"Go on, damn it!"

"Cuchillo has two squaws, he says, but he wants another. The granddaughter of our esteemed mayor."

Travis gripped Timoteo by the shoulder. "You're sure?"

There were tears in the big brown eyes as Travis gripped harder. "*Sí! Sí!* I would not lie. I was glad to escape with my life."

Travis looked at Jorge. "Cuchillo has seen Theresa?"

"Yes. In times of peace the Apaches came here to trade and barter. Cuchillo has seen her many times."

Timoteo nodded. "He knows her well."

Travis rubbed his jaw. "The message was for the mayor. I may as well tell him."

Travis went to the big house with Jorge, while Timoteo squatted on the porch. The old man was seated in his big chair when Travis and Jorge entered. Travis told him of what had happened.

James Morris fingered his ornate cane. "Jorge, tell Tomaso Quintana, Guillermo Castillo, Carlos Martinez and Jethro Arnold to come here at once."

"Yes, my mayor." Jorge hurried from the room.

"They are the leading men of the town," said James Morris. "We will decide what to do."

"There is only one thing to do – tell Cuchillo to go to hell!"

The old man raised his head. "I am the mayor," he said. "I cannot make decisions of my own without consulting the representatives of the people."

"Jesus," said Travis softly. He walked to a
249

window and looked out into the sunlit patio. Theresa was cutting flowers and placing them in a basket. The sun shone on her glossy dark hair.

The four men came breathlessly into the huge room. Quintana, Castillo, and Martinez were typical New Mexicans, while Jethro Arnold was a tall, gangling Anglo whose bones seemed to protrude through his flesh. His Adam's apple slid continuously up and down his long turkeylike throat.

James Morris explained the situation to the four men, and then patiently awaited their decision. Arnold was the first to speak. "Tell him to go to hell," he said in a nasal Yankee twang. "We've got guns and men who know how to use them. We've got soldiers here, too. The *torreon* is now strong again. No Apache in his right mind will buck up against determined men shooting from behind thick walls. What do you say, Captain?"

Travis nodded. "Cuchillo is bluffing."

Tomaso Quintana wet his lips. "No, he is not," he said quietly. "He has already killed some of our people. He has many warriors in the hills, well-armed and well-mounted. He has been but playing with us up until now. He means business, my mayor."

"So?" asked Travis.

"Let him have what he wants."

250

"Including Theresa?"

Tomaso flushed. "I did not say that."

"Guillermo Castillo," said Morris quietly.

Castillo was a plump man with darting eyes. "I agree with Tomaso Quintana," he said. "The soldiers will be of little help. Cuchillo can raid us at will. The girl is but a girl."

"Would you send your own granddaughter, Guillermo?" asked Jethro harshly.

Guillermo smiled. "Cuchillo does not want *her*," he said.

"Carlos Martinez?" asked Morris.

Martinez was a big man, lean and strong-looking, with a mahogany face with the look of a hawk upon it. "Fight!" he said loudly. "To the last wall! To the last cartridge! To the last man! Are we to pay tribute to that half-naked savage? We are men of men! Fight, I say!"

Morris bowed his head. "We can give him horses, mules, ammunition, guns and supplies. I cannot give up my granddaughter."

"It is for the common good," said Tomaso Quintana.

"After all," said Guillermo Castillo, spreading out his hands, "she *is* part Opata, is she not, my mayor?"

"That is true," said Tomaso.

"Be quiet!" snapped Jorge.

Morris looked toward Travis. "I am an old

251

man. There is no use in deluding myself otherwise. I can no longer make decisions. It is time for a younger man to take over. Captain Travis, will you meet and talk with Cuchillo under a flag of truce?"

"Him?" sneered Guillermo Castillo. "What has he to do with us?"

"He may be the means of saving your miserable bodies, if not your misbegotten souls," said Carlos Martinez. He raised a big hand over the head of Castillo. Castillo shrank away from the angry man.

Tomaso Quintana wet his thick lips. "There is no harm in the captain talking with Cuchillo, of course, providing Cuchillo will meet him."

Jorge held out a hand. "Timoteo Castro told me Cuchillo would come into the town to see our mayor."

Tomaso rubbed his throat. "Perhaps we could ambush him."

Martinez laughed. "*We?* You'll be under your bed when Cuchillo comes into our *placita*. Have you the courage, you squeaking mouse, to face Cuchillo, much less plunge a blade into his back?"

"It was but a suggestion," muttered Quintana.

Jethro Arnold paced back and forth like an ungainly stork. "Let Captain Walker meet and talk with Cuchillo. But the Apache must have a safe conduct."

"Pah!" said Guillermo Castillo.

James Morris thudded the tip of his cane against the floor. "So be it. You will do this for us, Captain?"

"I will be glad to. But suppose he will not negotiate? Suppose he insists upon having Theresa?"

"Theresa shall not go," said Martinez.

They all looked at each other, then at the blind mayor. Travis beckoned to Jorge Valadez. "Send Timoteo back to Cuchillo. Tell him to tell the chief that I will meet him at the edge of town on the road to the north, when the sun is at its highest. I will bear no arms and neither must he. Will I need an interpreter?"

"Baconora could interpret Apache but it will not be necessary, for Cuchillo speaks Spanish well."

"That's more than I can do. You will come along to help out perhaps?"

"I would go, but Baconora is your man."

"Yes, I think so. Besides, he knows the ways of those people better than any of us. He would be of great help."

"I will tell Timoteo and then go to find Baconora."

"It will do no good," said Tomaso Quintana

in a doleful voice. "We are under the thumbs of the Apaches."

"Shut up, you vermin!" roared Carlos Martinez.

Travis walked to the window again and looked out at the beautiful young woman he loved. There was a cold feeling in the pit of his belly as he looked at her and thought of the demand of Cuchillo Rojo.

Baconora looked up at the cloud-dotted sky. "It's about time," he said.

Travis nodded. He unbuckled his gun belt and handed it to Jorge, then unsnapped his carbine from its sling and gave it also to the Mexican. Baconora had already removed his weapons.

"Can he be trusted?" asked Travis.

"I wouldn't be going out there without weapons if he couldn't be," said the scout dryly.

"Seems strange a savage like him can be trusted in such matters."

Baconora filled his pipe and lit it. "They have their points of honor. Besides, it's to his advantage to talk with you to try and get his way. He doesn't want to lose any of his warriors if he can grease his way into what he wants."

Some of the townspeople watched Travis

curiously as he mounted his sorrel. Others of them stood on roof tops or atop the *torreon*. "There is dust on the road, Captain!" called one of the men on the *torreon*.

Travis uncased his field glasses and focused them on two approaching horsemen. They were Apaches, and one of them was Cuchillo Rojo. There was no mistaking the matted headdress and the two yellow-stained horns protruding from it. "Let's go," said Travis to Baconora.

They rode slowly out upon the rutted road. Two hundred yards from the last building Travis drew rein and waited for the two Mimbrenos to approach. There was no sign of weapons about them, but Travis knew they usually carried a short curved *besh*, or reserve knife, in their breechcloths.

The two warriors drew in their horses fifty yards from Travis and Baconora. Baconora held up a hand, palm toward the two warriors. Cuchillo responded the same way. The two Mimbrenos rode forward and sat their horses fifteen feet from the two white men. Travis studied the chief with interest. He was of medium height, but had the chest and shoulders of a wrestler. His mouth was thin, with the corners drawn down, while his hooked nose gave him the look of a predatory animal. His eyes were large, with

255

a basilisk look about them. A four-stranded medicine cord hung about his neck, strung with turquoise, petrified wood, rock crystal, eagle down, hawk and bear claws. Travis knew four-stranded medicine cords were rare among the Apaches and held great power for the wearer.

"How are you, my brother?" asked Baconora.

Cuchillo did not answer. His hard eyes studied Travis from head to foot.

Travis was annoyed. "Tell him we did not come out here to sweat under the sun."

Baconora spoke swiftly in slurring, gutteral Apache.

The hard eyes held Travis' eyes. "I speak Spanish," said the chief. "Does this white eagle speak it also?"

Travis nodded. "Well enough, Cuchillo Rojo."

"It is well. You have heard my demands. Why have you come out here to talk?"

"Because we do not intend to meet your demands."

"So? What is there to stop me from taking the town and everything in it?"

"The soldiers at Fort Joslyn."

The bluff did not work. There was a trace of amusement in the chief's voice as he spoke again. "So? They do not dare leave their walls and come out into the open to fight Cuchillo Rojo. I would sweep them to the Rio Grande like the flash floods of the high mountains."

"The chief talks big," said Travis quietly.

Cuchillo slapped a hand against his bare chest. "I own this country and everything in it. Fort Joslyn and Santa Theresa are mine. Go back into the town, white eagle, and have my supplies and the woman brought out here. I will give you until sundown."

"No," said Travis.

Cuchillo raised his big head. "There is nothing you can do to stop me. I have killed your messengers. I have run off your horses and mules. I have stopped you from using the roads. There are no more soldiers coming here. There are no soldiers between here and the Colorado. This I know. You cannot stay here, and you cannot escape. It is up to Cuchillo Rojo to decide what to do with you."

"You talk like the night wind in the mountains."

The mahogany-hued face tightened. The Mimbreno thrust out a clenched hand. "You have until sundown!"

Baconora puffed at his pipe. "Supposing we give you the supplies only?"

The proud head came up, and the eyes seemed to spark. "I want the supplies and the woman – all! *All!*"

Travis yawned. "There is a cannon at Fort Joslyn," he said. "If you attack us, Cuchillo Rojo, you will all die."

The chief spat into the road. "The white eagle has not been to his fort for some hours," he said harshly. "Perhaps he had better find out what has happened there before he threatens Cuchillo Rojo."

A cold feeling surged through Travis as he eyed the Mimbreno.

Baconora spoke out of the corner of his mouth. "He isn't pulling our legs, Captain. He's been up to some deviltry in the past few hours."

Cuchillo looked at the hills. "My warriors are ready for battle," he said. "Usen is on our side. Stenatliha, the mother of warriors, will be with us in the battle. You have until sundown, white eagle. Remember. *Yadalanh!*" He turned his apaloosa and rode off, followed by his companion.

Baconora tamped down the tobacco in his pipe. "Well?"

"He knows what he can do."

"Yeh. But he's got aces and kings, Captain."

"What the hell did you expect me to do? Give him the girl?"

"No, but how are you going to stop him from coming in and taking her?"

Travis turned his mount. As he did so he saw a pillar of smoke rising to the south, about where Fort Joslyn was situated. Baconora took his pipe from his mouth. He whistled softly. "By Jesus," he said, "maybe Cuchillo wasn't bluffing after all."

There was a dusty courier in the plaza when Travis and Baconora returned. He saluted Travis. "Sir, there's hell to pay at the fort. Some Apaches got close into the walls and set fire to the forage stacked behind the corrals and the quartermaster warehouse. Corporal Cole and five men were killed when they ran off the warriors and were ambushed. The major orders you back at once."

Travis nodded. "Can we get through?"

The trooper shrugged. "I didn't see a damned Apache on the way here, sir."

Travis rubbed his jaw. He looked up at the sun. Cuchillo wanted his answer by sundown or there would be hell to pay in Santa Theresa as well as Fort Joslyn.

Baconora looked at Travis. "We can make it to the fort and be back here in plenty of time, Captain."

"Let's go!" snapped Travis. He hated the thought of leaving now, but he was sure Cuchillo wouldn't attack the town until he was positive his demands would not be met. Travis hailed a trooper. "Tell Captain Cass he is in charge. Have him tell the mayor that I will be back before sundown. No one is to leave town and the guards are to be doubled. No man is to go about unless he is armed."

"Yes, sir!"

The courier led the way out of the town. Travis looked back at the mayor's house. He wanted desperately to see Theresa before he left, but he knew his duty was first to Fort Joslyn and second to the people of Santa Theresa.

The smoke was drifting off when the three riders debouched from the sandy pass to look toward the post. "Looks like the fire is out," said the courier.

"Yeh," said Baconora, "but look to the west."

Dust was drifting up from a flat area a mile west of the fort, and sunlight glistened from bright metal.

" 'Paches," said Baconora, "a whole Gawdammit mess of 'em, and they ain't out gathering cactus apples to make *hoosh.*"

"There's dust at the post too, sir," said the courier.

Dust spiraled up from near the gateway of the fort. A dozen troopers spurred their horses toward the Apaches. An officer led them on a fine black.

"DeSantis!" said Travis. "Come on! Shake the dung!"

They rode swiftly toward the post, but DeSantis and his men had too good a lead. Two hundred yards from the milling Apaches DeSantis drew his saber and yelled a command. The yelling troopers drew their pistols and sabers and shot forward into the dust, led by Norval DeSantis seeking the glory trail.

The Apaches parted before the onslaught of the troopers, letting them pass beyond the war party, and then the warriors closed in behind the troopers, cutting them off from the fort.

"They've had it now," said Baconora.

Dust coiled up from the beating of many hoofs. The sun glanced from deadly bright metal. Guns popped in the melee, and sabers rose and fell. The circling combatants moved farther and farther away from the fort, until a deep swell in the desert hid them from view but did not hide the dust. Hoarse yells and shrill whoopings were punctuated by the rattle of gunfire.

Travis drew rein a hundred yards from the fort. Troopers and infantrymen stood between the buildings with ready rifles and musketoons. The howitzer was manned and pointed toward the distant conflict. Major Lester stood to one side of it, bared sword in hand and Kossuth hat drawn tightly down to just above his eyes.

"Look!" said the courier.

A knot of hard-riding Apaches appeared above the rise of the dip in the desert, racing toward the post like brown centaurs. Travis drew his carbine around to rest it on his pommel as he cocked and capped it. Baconora raised his head. "Best get inside," he said.

They rode toward the gateway. The Apaches shot past the northern side of the fort. One of them hurtled something toward Travis and his two companions. Baconora jumped to one side as the rounded object thudded against the wall beside him.

"Jesus," said the trooper. He turned and retched violently.

Travis looked down at the dusty, bloody head of Norval DeSantis. The eyes were wide in the head, as though not comprehending what had happened to him.

"He got his Gawdammit cavalry charge," said Baconora.

The Apaches circled the post, yelling like furies. They raced across the knoll south of the fort and headed west toward the main body of warriors. Travis looked up to see Enos Lester flourish his sword. "Fire!" yelled the major.

A trooper jerked the lanyard. The friction

262

tube sparked and the brass howitzer belched flame and smoke. Then there was a grating, cracking sound and the roof of the warehouse collapsed. The major disappeared from sight inside the warehouse.

"Jesus God!" said Travis. "I knew that would happen."

The shot from the howitzer struck the desert floor a good fifty yards behind the yelling warriors, then bounded from sight amid the thick brush.

Baconora picked up the head which lay at his feet. He carried it into the quadrangle and snatched up a sack which lay over a railing. He covered the head and looked at Travis. "What the hell do I do with this now?"

Travis did not answer. He sprinted toward the warehouse. Clinton Vaughn and two men were trying to open the front door, which had been jammed by the collapse of the thick dirt roof. Vaughn looked back at Travis. Sweat dripped from his face. "Thank God a sane man has arrived," he said.

He pried the door open and walked into the dust-choked interior. A trooper lay beneath a beam, his sightless eyes staring at them. Another trooper sat back against the wall, nursing a shattered leg. Major Enos Lester lay across the broken trail of the howitzer, coated with thick dust. His sword had snapped at

263

the hilt, but he still held the handle in a shaking hand. He turned to look at Travis. "Mr. Travis," he choked. "Take command, sir. I have been mortally injured in the service of my country, sir."

"Get him out of here," said Travis in disgust.

They carried the sagging form of the major to his quarters. Medical orderlies took care of the injured trooper while four men carried out the dead man. Clinton Vaughn leaned against the wall. "My God," he said. "You would never have believed it, Travis."

"Let's get a drink."

They walked across the sunlit quadrangle. Men still stood with ready weapons, but there was no sign of the Apaches other than a dust wraith which drifted off before the wind.

Clint poured two big hookers. They downed them. "Tell me the details," said Travis quietly.

Clint wiped the sweat and dust from his face. "They fired the warehouse. I think they must have gotten close to the walls last night and hid themselves under blankets and sand until they had a chance to fire it. Corporal Cole and five men went after them and were cut down within sight of all of us. DeSantis bullied the major into letting him go after the Apaches."

"I saw what happened," said Travis quietly.

Clint refilled his glass and downed the potent liquor. "What do we do now?"

"Cuchillo Rojo has demanded supplies, guns and ammunition from the people of Santa Theresa. In return he'll let the town alone."

"Why don't they let him have them?"

"There's more to it than that, Clint. He also wants Theresa Morris as his squaw."

Clint paled. "You're fooling me, Travis!"

"No."

"My God. How long has he given them?"

"Until sundown."

"You'll have to tell the major."

"I've got more than that to tell him. We should abandon this fort and garrison Santa Theresa instead."

"He has his orders."

"Yes, but he'd better damned well start making decisions to get himself out of this mess."

There was a rap at the door. "Come in," said Clint.

Kelligan, Major Lester's orderly, opened the door. His face was pale and drawn. "Sir," he said thickly to Travis, "you'd better come at once to the major's quarters."

"What's happened?"

"The major just blew out his brains, sir."

CHAPTER FOURTEEN

Martin Newkirk was standing in the major's quarters, holding a sheaf of papers in his hands, as Travis and Clint entered. His face was pale as he nodded toward the door that opened into the duplicate set of quarters on the far side of the hallway. "He's in there," he said quietly.

Travis opened the door. Major Lester lay across a roped trunk. His service pistol lay on the dusty floor below his hanging right hand. Blood had wormed its way around the corner of the trunk, and made a rivulet on the floor. The major's head was hanging on the far side of the trunk. Travis looked about. The walls were hung with family pictures and pictures of the major in uniform at various stages of his forty years of service, from a fresh-faced cadet at the Academy to a picture which could not have been taken more than several years before.

Travis shut the door and walked into the major's quarters. Newkirk raised his head. "I came in here to see if he was all right. The old man seemed stunned and broken, as though he had suffered a terrible blow. His

266

very face sagged. He looked at me as though he had never seen me before, and asked me what I wanted. I brought his attention to these orders I have in my hands. Then he said a very curious thing . . ."

"Go on," prompted Travis.

"He said he knew I had found out about him and that there was no use in his carrying on the masquerade. He asked me to wait here, and then he walked into those quarters across the hall. A moment later I heard the report of his pistol. I looked in and saw that he was dead, and sent Kelligan to tell you, Captain."

"What are those orders?"

Newkirk wet his dry lips. "They had been sent to Major Lester by Colonel Canby, dated June sixteenth of this year, ordering him to abandon Fort Joslyn, to remove his command and all government property to Fort Craig. In addition he was to afford military protection for the inhabitants of Santa Theresa who wished to evacuate the town and travel to the Rio Grande. The orders contain an appendix to the effect that the major must declare martial law and order the evacuation of Santa Theresa or the government would not be responsible for the safety of the inhabitants."

Travis stared at the adjutant. "Did you know about this before?"

"No. The orders were kept in the major's

267

private file. It always seemed peculiar to me that we at Fort Joslyn were left out here on the edge of nowhere, when all the other posts were abandoned. The major seemed to be holding something back from me."

"He sure was," said Clint dryly. "Maybe he held it back just *too* long."

Martin Newkirk took off his spectacles. "Captain Travis, do you remember me remarking about the major's order for you to remain here?"

"Yes."

"He had no right to do so. Included in this sheaf of orders was one which was sent to Major Lester a week or so before you got here. He had specific orders to speed you on your way to Fort Craig and thence to Sante Fe. There was also a peremptory order for him to follow his instructions as laid down in the preceding order of June sixteenth, and a request for an immediate reply as to why he had not complied with those orders."

"Jesus," breathed Clint. "Why did he conceal those orders?"

Martin Newkirk wiped his glasses and replaced them on his nose. "I think I can guess why," he said quietly. "Major Lester knew how he stood in the department. He knew there was little chance of his ever receiving any type of field command again.

268

He would be relegated to paper work again, as he had always been. Perhaps he thought he would establish a reputation as a field soldier and eventually get his regiment or brigade."

"But the man was incapable of command in the field," said Clint. "Why would he deliberately seek such duty?"

"I don't really know," said the adjutant. "The major probably felt that he had been a failure all during his forty years of service and perhaps thought he might redeem himself, although he probably knew it was a hopeless task. Still, he was like a dog in the manger, fighting to save what rank he had."

Travis nodded. "You've hit it there, Newkirk."

"What are your orders, sir?" asked Newkirk.

Clint nodded. "Your whole staff is here, Captain."

Clint's words were like a dash of icy water on Travis. He had forgotten that the three of them were all that was left of the original complement of officers at Fort Joslyn. Major Lester had died by his own hand in disgrace; Ken Carlie had been shot to death by Travis as a traitor; Norval DeSantis had died in a mad charge against the Mimbrenos; Charles Cass was on detached duty in Santa Theresa and was up to God knew what deviltry.

"Well, Travis?" asked Clint.

Travis walked to the window and looked out upon the sunny quadrangle. His duty was clear. Fort Joslyn should have been abandoned weeks ago. Perhaps now it was too late, but there was nothing he could do about that except to try his best to get his new command and the people of Santa Theresa back to the safety of Fort Craig. Then there was the matter of Cuchillo Rojo, who within the next five or six hours would close in on Santa Theresa, safe in the belief that he could override and despoil it with little or no opposition.

"We're waiting, sir," said Martin Newkirk.

Travis turned and eyed the two serious officers. He needed more shoulder straps, but these two would have to do. "Clint," he said, "you'll have to remove enough supplies from the warehouse to feed and clothe the command for at least two weeks. I don't have to go into detail. You're quartermaster, and a damned practical man to boot. You'll know what to do.

"Martin, I want you to destroy all papers which are not important. Vital papers will be transported with us. When you have taken care of that you will prepare the command for movement to Santa Theresa. Each man is to carry forty rounds, a full canteen, and

270

nothing else beyond his rifle or musketoon. The civilians will strip down to essentials. Every civilian man on the post will march with the wagon guard. Do you think you can handle it? You're really a paper-work soldier, I'm afraid."

Clint grinned. "Don't worry about Marty, Travis. Beneath that scholarly exterior there beats the heart of a real field soldier who hates paper work and likes to hear the whistle of rifle balls and smell the stink of burnt powder."

Travis bent his head. "Hop to it then. Shake the dung. I want to be in Santa Theresa no later than an hour before sundown."

Clint whistled softly. Newkirk wiped his brow. Travis took the orders from the adjutant's hand. "I'll take charge of these," he said.

The two officers saluted and left Travis alone. Travis scanned through the orders and mentally cursed the dead man in the next room. The egotistical little failure had almost doomed scores of people to death.

The sun was slanting low in the western sky when the convoy was made up in the post quadrangle. Sweating, cursing men finished up the last details. A great pile of furniture, blankets, tents, cases of supplies

271

and foodstuffs lay in the center of the quadrangle. A powder train had been laid just outside the quartermaster warehouse, and it led to several kegs of powder in the center of the heaped supplies buried under the collapsed roof.

The cavalry stood to horse, booted and spurred. Minutes before, they had done the most painful duty a mounted soldier can perform – killing the horses and mules that were too weak for the forthcoming trip across the country to the Rio Grande.

Noncoms went from building to building, making sure nothing was left in them which could be used by the Apaches. Axes rang as they cut through the spokes of extra wagons that could not be taken along. Like most men, the troopers seemed to have taken a perverse delight in the work of destruction after they had been told what material was to be taken along and what was to be destroyed to prevent its being used by the enemy. Now and then the crashing of glass punctured the sharp strokes of the axes.

Travis walked along the line of barracks, taking the reports of the noncoms. "All clear, sir."

Travis reached the head of the column. He looked about the fort. Already it had a curiously lonely look about it. "Prepare to mount!" commanded Travis. "Mount!"

Troopers rose and smashed down into the leather of their saddles. Teamsters mounted to the wagon boxes.

"Forwa-ard ho!" called out Travis.

The advance detail of eight cavalrymen under a corporal moved out smartly. The lead wagons pulled out with a line of plodding infantrymen on each side. Dust roiled up from the big wheels as the whole line of wagons got into motion. Then followed the rear guard of a squad of infantrymen followed by a squad of cavalrymen. The rear guard cleared the gate. Clinton Vaughn looked at Travis. "Now?"

Travis nodded.

Clint pulled down the United States flag, folded it, and placed it in one of his saddlebags. He looked again at Travis.

"Fire the train," said Travis.

Clint knelt and broke off a match from a block he held in his hand. He touched off the powder train. It fizzled and sputtered, making swift speed along the heaped black line of powder. Travis took the block of matches and broke off a match. He lit the whole block and tossed it onto the oilsoaked pile of torn blankets and uniforms at one side of the big pile on the parade ground. It caught at once and began to chew into the pile of abandoned goods.

Travis and Clint mounted and rode past the two gate buildings. "How long?" asked Clint.

"Ten or fifteen minutes. The powder train is long enough."

"You don't think the Apaches will attack the wagon train?"

"With the post abandoned before their eyes? They'll be in for loot before too long."

The bitter dust of the wagons' passage swirled about them. There was no sign of life out on the desert, but both men knew the Apaches were out there, watching the curious actions of the white-eyes.

The two officers reached the rear guard and rode silently along with it. Travis looked back. A pall of smoke was rising against the late afternoon sky, dotted with fat sparks that winked in and out of the streamers of smoke.

There was a movement out in the mesquite, and a group of Apaches rode slowly toward the fort. The wind shifted and the smoke blew toward them. They increased their pace, and in a few minutes were within fifty yards of the post.

"The powder train must have burned out," said Clint.

Travis shrugged. As he did so there was a hollow booming noise, and a cloud of smoke and flame shot up into the air, dotted with fragments of supplies and adobe. A wash of

274

gas and flame met the oncoming Apaches and shut them from view. The explosion echoed faintly from the distant hills.

Clint Vaughn grinned. "Well," he said, "they got their damned loot – right in their greasy faces."

The wagons ground into the plaza of Santa Theresa, and came to a halt in swirling dust as the sun seemed to rest motionless atop the western hills. Clint Vaughn saluted Travis. "What are the captain's orders?"

"Find Captain Cass and notify him that I have taken command. Find quarters for the civilians we have brought with us. Incorporate the temporary garrison here into the troops who came with us. The wagons will be placed in a defensive square here in the center of the plaza. All horses and mules are to be placed in the town corral and a double guard placed over them."

A burst of drunken laughter came from a nearby *cantina*. Travis looked toward it. "Have Mr. Newkirk post a notice to the effect that Santa Theresa is now under martial law. As of sunset tonight all *cantinas* will be closed to business until I order otherwise."

"Yes, sir."

Travis dismounted. "I'll go to see the mayor."

Clint looked up at the dying sun. "It's almost time, Travis."

Travis crossed the dusty plaza and rapped on the outer door of the Morris *casa*. Angelique opened the door. Her face was red and swollen. "Thank the good God you are here," she said brokenly.

"What is wrong, Angelique?"

"Theresa ... Theresa ... my God, I cannot say it, *capitán*."

"Speak!"

"She is gone."

Travis gripped the woman by her shoulders. "Gone? Where?"

"We do not know. Captain Cass came here and spoke to her. She left the house with that swine. Esteban told me later she had been wearing her riding habit."

Travis pushed passed the sobbing woman. He hurried into the great room where James Morris usually sat. The old man looked up at him. "Where has Theresa gone?" asked Travis.

"I do not know. I do not understand how or why she would leave with that man. She did not say anything to me, her own grandfather."

"I brought back the troops to defend the town against Cuchillo. We had until sundown to meet his demands."

The old man bowed his head. "She was

276

gone so quickly we had no time to talk with her. It is said they were seen riding south from the town, but it was Timoteo Castro who saw them, and Timoteo is known as a great liar who likes attention and will tell wild tales to gain it."

Travis hurried from the room and looked about the deserted patio. He went to her room and opened the door. Her waist and flowing skirt lay on the floor beside the little beaded moccasins she usually wore.

A shadow darkened the floor beside Travis. He turned to look into the eyes of Evelyn Cass. "Do you know anything about this?" he asked, pointing to the clothing on the floor.

She shrugged. "She left town with Charlie, although how he talked her into it is beyond me."

There was a cold feeling within Travis. "But why?"

She leaned against the side of the doorway. "You don't know Charlie very well, Travis. You shamed him more than once. He knew you loved Theresa, and, although he could do nothing about that, he wanted revenge."

"But where did he take her?"

She looked away. Travis gripped her by the shoulders and shook her. "You'll tell me," he said harshly, "or I'll break your pretty neck."

Her eyes held his, and there seemed to be a

glint of malice in them. "I think he's taken her to Cuchillo Rojo," she said.

He dropped his hands. "I don't believe it."

"No? I'm sure he has. Charlie knew you'd turn in a report against him. He knew his army career would end if you did so. Perhaps he thought he'd gain favor with Cuchillo by bringing Theresa to him. I don't know. There was always a touch of madness in Charlie. Only I knew it. This is just the type of revenge he'd seek against you, Travis."

Travis pushed past her.

"Where are you going?"

"After her."

She gripped his right arm. "No, Travis! Let them go! Why risk your life for her?"

Travis turned. "I don't think you'd understand why I would risk my life for Theresa. It's beyond your comprehension."

She came closer to him. "Travis, forget about her. She can't give you anything. Charlie is gone. He'll never come back. Am I so unattractive to you?"

He walked away. "You pick the damnedest times to get romantic," he said over his shoulder.

The sun was gone when Travis found Clint Vaughn. "Cass has taken Theresa away," said Travis. Evelyn says he has taken Theresa to Cuchillo Rojo."

Clint paled. "She's lying!"

"I don't think so."

"What can we do?"

Travis looked at the darkening hills to the west. "I'm going after her."

"I'll get the men ready."

"No. A detachment would never make it, Clint. There's a slim chance I might get through alone. If I don't get back the command is yours. It's a big responsibility, but if you get through to Fort Craig there will be a promotion in it for you."

"Damn the promotion!"

Baconora came through the darkness to them. "You're going after Theresa, Captain?" he asked quietly.

"Yes."

"I'll go with you. I know where Cuchillo's camp is."

"You realize the odds against us?"

Baconora grinned crookedly. "I've had odds against me before. Besides, I'd rather take my chances out there than sit around here and wait for the 'Paches to gobble us up. A man would have a chance to get away out there. If Cuchillo hits Santa Theresa there might not be a man left to tell the tale."

"Cheerful beggar," said Clint dryly.

"I call them the way I figure them," said the scout.

Travis sent a trooper for his horse. He looked again at the dark hills. He might be able to save the girl. Perhaps if he killed Cuchillo the strength of the Apache force would be lost. It had happened before when a good leader was killed. But the odds of Travis getting out alive were stacked high against him.

First Sergeant Mack Ellis knocked on the outer door of the Morris *casa*. The door swung open under the blows of his big fist. There were no lights in the house. Ellis walked down the long corridor which led to the patio. The house seemed deserted until he reached the patio and saw a light in one of the bedrooms. He crossed to it and rapped on the door.

"Who is it?" called out Evelyn Cass.

Ellis felt a surge of heat go through his big body as he heard her voice. "It's Sergeant Ellis, Mrs. Cass," he said. "I'm looking for the captain."

She opened the door. "I think he has left town," she said.

"Left town, ma'am? I don't understand."

She eyed the big noncom. Maybe this was her chance. She had noticed the way Ellis looked at her. "I think the captain has pulled out on the rest of us," she said.

"I don't believe that!"

280

"No?" She tilted her shapely head to one side. "Captain Walker knows that Santa Theresa is doomed. Theresa Morris has been taken by my husband to the camp of Cuchillo. At least I think that is what he has done."

Ellis was bewildered. "But why?"

"My husband hates Captain Walker. It is a form of revenge for my husband. Captain Walker said he was going to find Theresa Morris, but I don't believe him at all. I think he has deserted us to make for the Rio Grande, don't you?"

"He mentioned a couple of times that he wished he had gone on to the river alone."

She nodded. "I don't want to stay here, Sergeant, and die under some greasy warrior's hand, nor do I want to have the last bullet for myself. Do you understand?"

Ellis shook his head. She placed a hand on his arm. "Listen," she said quietly. "Cuchillo will attack Santa Theresa. We have no chance here if he does. I want to get out of here. You know the country. Take me away from here, Sergeant."

"He looked down at her. She was a real filly, all right. He had thought of her many times at Fort Joslyn. She pressed close to him. "You will, won't you?"

"It would be desertion," he said.

"Look, Sergeant – no one will know. In

281

time Santa Theresa will be wiped out. You know that as well as I do. Think of what a feather it would be in your cap if you saved an officer's wife from the Apaches."

Ellis swallowed thickly. She raised her face to his. He drew her close within his big arms and kissed her. Her arms crept about his neck, and he felt her press close to him. She withdrew her lips. Ellis looked at the bed and lifted her from her feet, but she pressed her hands against his flushed face. "No," she whispered. "Not now. We haven't time. You'll get everything you want when we reach the Rio Grande."

"But you're an officer's wife," he said anxiously.

She smiled. "A man like you won't always be an enlisted man," she said. "I'll talk to your superior officers. After saving my life, surely they'll consider you for a commission."

"Yeah," he said. He looked up. "Yeah. By God, you've hit it."

"Get horses and food. Hurry now." She kissed him again.

Ellis hurried off. She leaned against the side of the door, watching him, wrinkling her nose at the sour sweat odor of him, which still clung about her. "My God," she said. She laughed. "The poor damned fool."

The desert was shrouded in darkness, and the wind swept across it, rustling sage and mesquite. Now and then Baconora stopped to listen. Travis looked ahead toward the dim brooding bulk of the hills. The scout had said he knew where Cuchillo's camp was situated.

Baconora turned to Travis. "We'd best ride north toward the end of the hills, then turn in behind them toward Cuchillo's camp. They won't expect anyone coming that way."

"How long will it take?"

"What difference does that make? We sure as hell won't be able to get close to his camp coming this way."

"Lead on, then."

They rode to the north. After twenty minutes Baconora halted. "Listen," he said.

Above the rushing of the night wind they heard the muffled beating of hoofs. They slid from their mounts and led them down into an arroyo. Travis stayed with the horses while Baconora dropped at the edge of the arroyo. In a few minutes he came to Travis. "Big war party," he whispered. "Heading toward Santa Theresa."

"Did you see Cuchillo?"

"No. Leastways I didn't see any buck wearing a horned headdress, and I know damned well Cuchillo won't go anywhere without that headdress. It's big medicine for him. It's my thought that Cuchillo has sent his warriors ahead to lay siege to the town."

Travis nodded. "I wonder if he's still in those hills?"

"There's only one way to find out, Captain."

"Let's go, then."

They rode on to the north.

Sergeant Mack Ellis already had his misgivings. The woman rode silently behind him, her face muffled in a silk scarf. The dark hills were to their left as they rode for the old stage road north of Santa Theresa. Ellis had thought he might catch up with Travis Walker and Baconora, but now he knew he had been mistaken. It was too dark for him to see much of anything. It would be daylight before they found a place of shelter. There were many miles between them and the Rio Grande. He glanced back at her. She had played him for the fool, leading him on into desertion, with payment of a few kisses and a vague promise of other favors.

"Do you know where you are?" she asked sharply.

"Yes."

"You're lying."

He turned to look at her. "Maybe you'd rather go back?"

284

"No!"

"All right then." He spurred his horse and rode on.

The eastern sky was alight with the false dawn as Travis and Baconora rode through malpais country, torn and tumbled masses of rock mingled with ocotillo, catclaw and mesquite. The wind had shifted and now came from the east. Travis looked up at the rough hills. "I thought we'd be closer than this by now," he said. "Damn it, man, I thought you knew this country!"

"I do," said Baconora quietly, from behind Travis. "That's why I came this way."

"We can't ride up those slopes now. They'd see us before we even got within carbine range."

"Exactly."

Travis turned quickly. Baconora's rifle rested across his left forearm, pointing at Travis' chest. Baconora cocked the heavy weapon with his right thumb, then curled his forefinger about the trigger. "I'll trouble you to get off that horse, Walker," he said.

"What does this mean?"

Baconora grinned. "Now you didn't really think I was loco enough to come out here with you on a wild goose chase after that girl, knowing damned well neither of us would ever leave here alive?"

Travis looked into the scout's hard reddish eyes. "What's your game, Baconora?"

Baconora looked up toward the hills. "The Army hasn't got a chance out here any more. There are no troops between here and the Colorado, and precious little chance of them ever being out there in the next few years. The Apaches are lords of Arizona and western New Mexico now – yeah, and clear down to Durango, too.

"A wise man will play along with the Apaches. I know Cuchillo. He'll reward me for my help. Silver, gold, women – anything I ask."

"He'll kill you at sight."

Baconora shook his shaggy head. "No. He can use me."

"What happens to me?"

Baconora spat. "Part of the deal with him was to bring you to him. He knew as long as you were around there'd be resistance. I've kept my word."

Travis studied the lean scout. "You've been in contact with him all along, then?"

Baconora nodded. "Just about. Get off that horse. Gather some mesquite. It's almost dawn. I want a signal fire started."

Travis dismounted and began to gather

286

mesquite branches. The mesquite crackled steadily.

"Throw some brush on it," ordered Baconora. "I want smoke."

Soon a streamer of smoke arose from the fire. Baconora sat down on a rock, always keeping his rifle pointing at Travis. "Unbuckle your gun belt," he said. "Throw it over here."

Travis did as he was told. There was no sign of life in the hills, but as he looked to the east he saw dust rising. His heart seemed to skip a beat.

Baconora suddenly laughed. "I'm thinking of that damned fool Cass," he said. "He was stupid enough to think Cuchillo would make the same kind of a deal with him that he made with me. Now Cuchillo probably has the girl. I wonder if she saw how Cass died."

"You think he's dead then?"

"Yeah. But if he ain't, he might as well be after Cuchillo gets through carving him up. Hawww!"

The sky was much lighter now. The wind shifted a little. The smoke drifted toward the quiet hills. Travis eyed the scout, hoping for a break, but Baconora was too wary.

Baconora stood up. "Look," he said. "We got company."

Travis turned. Two riders were

approaching them. One was a soldier, the other a woman. Baconora grinned. "It's that Cass filly and that damned fool of a first sergeant, Mack Ellis."

Travis turned as though warned by some subtle sense. He started a little. A group of Apaches had materialized up the slope from them. Even as Travis watched he saw most of the warriors lash their horses down the slope and start off at a long swinging pace toward the two riders east of the fire.

Baconora spat. "Damned fools," he said.

Travis could see the horned headdress on one of the Apaches who had not ridden after Mack Ellis and Evelyn Cass. There were two other Apaches with him and another rider, slight of figure, who rode just behind the chief. He knew it was Theresa.

"This oughta be good," said Baconora. "That stiff-backed sergeant is goin' to get his come-uppance."

Travis turned. The Apaches had spread out into a crescent and were closing in on the two riders. Mack Ellis swung down from his horse and shot it with his pistol. He turned to Evelyn Cass, but the woman sat bolt upright on her horse, staring at the painted death which was swooping down at her. Then she screamed and turned her horse to urge it back to the east. Mack Ellis yelled at her above the thudding of the hoofs. He raised his musketoon and fired at a leading Apache. The warrior went down. Carbines and rifles flatted off and the big sergeant went down on one knee.

The Apaches ringed the sergeant. Slugs rapped into him. Evelyn Cass was racing through the brush, followed by half a dozen screaming Apaches. Mack Ellis dropped another Apache with his pistol. He fired again and dropped a warrior's horse. He turned to look for the woman who had led him into a death trap.

Somehow Evelyn Cass had broken away from her pursuers. She lashed at her horse as she tried to reach Mack Ellis. Her long hair had broken free and streamed behind her as she rode.

Baconora spat. "She led that poor bastard to his death," he said. "At that, he's better off than she is. Wait until they get their hands on her."

Travis looked up the slope. Cuchillo sat his apaloosa, watching the fight on the flats below him. He was not looking toward the fire. Travis glanced at Baconora. The scout was watching the fight with avid interest. "Damn!" he said. "Ellis got another one of 'em!"

Travis' right hand closed on a rock. Two

swift strides took him close to Baconora. The scout whirled in time to get hit full in the face with the rock. He gasped as blood streamed from his nose and mouth. Travis jerked the rifle from the scout's hands and clubbed Baconora over the head. Baconora went down, spraying blood on the sand and rocks. Travis raised the rifle once more and drove the steel shod butt down in a smashing blow to the base of Baconora's neck, breaking his spine.

Travis snatched up his gun belt and buckled it hastily about his waist. He looked up the slope. Cuchillo was still watching the hopeless fight. Guns popped like grease in a big skillet. Travis got his Sharps and capped it. He took Baconora's rifle and placed it atop a flat rock. He got the scout's Colt and thrust it through his belt. As an afterthought, he took off the scout's blood-spattered hat and put it on his own head.

Mack Ellis was almost through. Evelyn Cass was trying to reach him. A warrior shot in close beside her and gripped her streaming hair. Mack Ellis turned. He raised his Colt and fired at her. She jerked and slid from her horse, and the hoofs of the warrior's horse thudded against her body.

Travis looked away as the Apaches closed in on the big sergeant. There was nothing he could do to help Mack Ellis.

Cuchillo was riding down the slope, followed by his two warriors and Theresa. The smoke drifted in between Travis and the little party. He stepped behind a big rock and gripped his carbine tightly in his hands. Three to one. The odds were high, and what he had to do he must do before the Apaches on the flats below rejoined their chief. But they'd worry the bodies of the two dead people in childish fury. That would give him a slim margin of time – a last desperate throw of the dice for life or death.

CHAPTER FIFTEEN

Cuchillo guided his gaudy apaloosa down the rough slope. It was then that Travis Walker saw the rope the chief held in his right hand, the other end of which was tied to Theresa's horse. Theresa was very pale and wan in the gray light of dawn.

Three Apaches were fifty yards from the arroyo when Travis fired his Sharps, dropping the right hand warrior instantly with a bullet through the heart. The other warrior's horse reared, and a slug from Baconora's rifle took the horse in the chest. The horse pitched as he came down, throwing his rider to the ground, pinning him helplessly against sharp-edged rocks.

Cuchillo jerked at the rope he held and tried to turn his apaloosa, but Travis Walker was clearing rocks as he raced toward the chief. The smoke drifted between them. Cuchillo dropped the rope and reached for his rifle, but Travis fired his Colt. He missed, but the slug sang thinly past Cuchillo's ear and startled him. Theresa took her cue. She dug her heels into the sides of the pony she rode and the mount carried her into the thick brush.

Travis stumbled and went down on one knee. He fired up at the chest of the apaloosa as Cuchillo drove the horse at him. Travis darted to one side, gripped the chief's right leg and upended him out of the Mexican saddle he rode. Cuchillo went down heavily on the far side of the horse. The apaloosa streaked for the flats, leaving Travis and Cuchillo face to face.

Cuchillo fired his pistol but Travis was under it, gripping the gun wrist with his left hand, forcing the gun higher and higher. Travis grunted in pain as Cuchillo's knee drove up into his groin. Travis fell backward, dragging the chief down on top of him. Cuchillo lost his pistol and swiftly drew out his knife. Travis jerked his head, striking it against a rock. He weakened as the knife came toward him. There was a muffled explosion behind Cuchillo, and his body jerked spasmodically. His mouth opened and blood flooded from it, splattering Travis. Cuchillo fell sideways as powder smoke blew toward Travis. Travis looked up into Theresa's pale face. She held a heavy pistol in her slim hands.

Travis rolled the dead chief aside. He stood up and drew her close. He heard a whooping cry out on the flats. He looked over her head and saw the Apaches closing in on the arroyo. Travis pushed the girl behind a rock and swiftly reloaded the rifle and carbine. He took the pistols and jumped behind a rock ledge.

There were five bucks coming in on the arroyo. Travis grinned. This was his meat. The rifle spoke and took one of the bucks through the head. Travis fired the carbine and downed another warrior. The other three quirted their horses off through the brush just as the sun showed itself over the eastern heights.

Travis slid an arm about Theresa's waist. "Let's go home," he said quietly.

CHAPTER SIXTEEN

Travis Walker stood up in his stirrups and waved his hat toward the east. "Move out! Forwa-ard ho!" he commanded.

The advance party of cavalry moved out at a smart trot, followed by the wagons and carts of the civilians. Behind the civilian wagons were the army vehicles. The wagon train was followed by a rear guard of cavalry, white lines of infantry and armed civilians plodded along each side of the column.

Travis looked about the quiet plaza after the rear guard had moved out. The dust was settling on the deserted buildings. There was a somber, lonely look about the old town. Beyond the town a tall wind devil rose on the sand flats, then moved toward Santa Theresa to sweep across the empty plaza and past the sagging *torreon*.

Clint Vaughn reined in his horse beside Travis. "I wonder how long the Apaches will let this place alone?"

"*Quién sabe?* They don't like ghost towns, Clint. This might be considered bad medicine for them. Maybe they'll stay away from it."

"Some day the Army will come back here.

Until then this is Apacheria, and God help the traveler who tries to cross it."

Travis nodded. He looked at the heat-hazy hills. "I wonder how Ben Joad is making out up there," he said.

"He's in good company . . . for *him*."

Travis touched his horse with his spurs. They did not look back as they followed the column out onto the dusty road.

The people talked in low voices as they moved about inside the circle of wagons. The firelight glinted dully from gun barrels as sentries paced along the outer rim of the wagons, and a scarf of smoke hung low over the camp. In the distance, Massacre Peak loomed up against the dark sky.

Travis Walker stood with his back to a wagon, looking out into the darkness. Clint Vaughn came to him. "How far are we from the river?" he asked.

"About twenty-five miles."

Clint looked to the west. "Odd that we haven't seen an Apache since we left Santa Theresa."

"There may be some ahead of us."

A sentry suddenly raised his rifle. "Halt!" he called. "Who goes there?"

"Friend!" the cracked voice sounded from the darkness.

"Advance to be recognized."

A man came out of the thick brush, weaving a little as he walked, leading a blown horse.

"Who are you?" called the sentry.

"Benson Duryea, courier from Fort Craig."

Travis ran toward the tired man and gripped him by the shoulders. "Thank God you made it, Duryea!"

The Kentuckian looked up. "I reached the river all right," he said. "They wanted to send another man back, but I insisted on coming back myself. My horse is almost gone. I ain't feeling too spry myself. I ain't sure I would have made it to Fort Joslyn, sir. Thank God I met you."

"What's the news, Duryea?" asked Clint.

"A strong reconnaissance party is following me. They should be bivouacked near Sunday Cone. They had orders to try and contact Fort Joslyn, sir. According to the commanding officer of Fort Craig, Fort Joslyn and Santa Theresa should have been abandoned weeks ago."

Travis nodded. Clint helped Duryea toward the wagons. Duryea turned. "Another thing, sir. I was told you were promoted to major and assigned to Canby's staff."

"Thanks, Duryea."

Travis walked into the center of the wagon circle. "We're safe now," he said. "We'll meet fresh troops some time tomorrow. The road is open to the Rio Grande and Fort Craig." He walked toward Theresa's wagon.

Theresa stood beside the wagon with her shawl over her dark hair. Travis took her in his arms. "We'll make Fort Craig now," he said. "How is your grandfather?"

She glanced at the wagon. "He has hardly said a word since we left Santa Theresa."

"He'll be back there some day."

She looked up at him and shook her head. "No," she said softly. "He'll never see it again, Travis. He spoke of it a little while ago, saying he'd never see Santa Theresa again, but that he was happy for me, knowing that we loved each other."

Travis looked to the east. "This will be a long war," he said.

She rested her head on his chest. "It will pass more quickly than you think, Travis, and then we'll have a long happy life ahead of us."

He raised her head and kissed her. The wind blew across the camp, fluttering the wagon tilts and driving the smoke of the campfires ahead of it. Far to the west the wind swept across Santa Theresa, raising whorls of dust on the empty plaza and moaning through the empty buildings. A coyote crept furtively across the plaza. A stone fell from the old *torreon*. Santa Theresa seemed to be waiting,

297

patiently waiting for its people to come back and bring it to life again. There was plenty of time. Santa Theresa dreamed on under the dark sky.